SARA & THE MAD DOG

PRAISE FOR STEPHEN MERTZ

"Stephen Mertz writes a hard-edged, fast-paced thriller for those who like their tales straight and sharp."
—Joe R. Lansdale, Bestselling author of *Hap & Leonard* series

"One of the best writers in the genre who deserves to be much more than the genre's best kept secret. A born storyteller!"
—Max Allan Collins, NYT Bestselling author of *Road to Perdition*

"One of the best adventure writers of our time!"
—*NYT* Bestselling writer James Reasoner

"Mertz is an action specialist!"
—*Ellery Queen's Mystery Magazine*

"The cleanest, strongest prose in the business."
—*Gravetapping.com*

SARA & THE MAD DOG

STEPHEN MERTZ

WOLFPACK
PUBLISHING
— EST 2013 —

For Michael "Hoodoo" Hyatt, who is everything a best friend should be.

CHAPTER ONE

February 7, 1932

A BREEZE BRUSHED Sara Carter's left shoulder ever so faintly where no breeze should have been.

The fatigue of travel had her in its grip, the result of an inability to catch even a fitful night's rest aboard trains. The night train from Memphis proved to be no exception. And here it was early morning in the grand, ornate lobby of the Waldorf-Astoria, the beginning of a new day, and she was plumb tuckered out. Their little group of three was waiting at the tail end of a line of arrivals and check-outs queued before a broad front desk behind which clerks were taking their own sweet time.

The Waldorf's lobby was every bit as crowded, noisy and busy as had been Grand Central Station thirty minutes earlier when Sara, AP, and her cousin Maybelle, who was also her best friend and sister-in-law, had stepped off the Midnight Flyer. Their recording trio, the Carter Family, returning to once again toil in the cold concrete world of Yankee land.

Sara and Maybelle had decided to take a load off while

AP signed them in, settling side by side on a sofa against a marble column facing the front desk, their modest assortment of mismatched luggage neatly arranged on the carpeted floor beside Maybelle. AP, Sara's husband, tall, gaunt and somber, was gradually inching forward, no longer at the end of the queue.

They were in high cotton, booked to perform in Carnegie Hall. At least the weather was in accord. Sara had endured Yankee winters before—the biting wind howling through skyscraper canyons, billowing accumulations of icy blowing snow. But on this day, according to the weather forecast, New York City was to continue enjoying its "heat wave," the nights cold but with mild, sunny, spring-like days. It wouldn't last but was nothing to complain about. And the topper on this visit...they were checking into New York's leading luxury hotel at the promoter's expense.

Though its doors had been open for business a mere three-and-a-half months, the elegant atmosphere pulsated with vibrant newness. The Waldorf-Astoria was already of significant renown worldwide, a grand hotel that could almost make one forget that the world's economy had crashed into a devastating Depression. It was said to be the tallest and largest hotel in the world with 2,200 rooms occupying an entire city block, a social center and a center of commerce with its row of elevators, a grand main entrance, stairways, and escalators. All manner of small businesses lined the lobby, brimming with customers. There was a beauty shop, barbershop, and small stores ranging from haberdasheries and shops of women's apparel to small eateries, a cigar store, and a "tea room" where liquor was discreetly served despite Prohibition still being the law of the land.

Sara had long ago learned to ignore the curious sideways glances of passersby, especially from womenfolk, in the big city. Easy enough to understand. She and Maybelle were wearing their Sunday best but there could be little doubt to those city women that she and Maybelle were from the country. City women always dressed more fashionably.

Yes indeed, they must have looked quite the pair what with Maybelle sitting erect, her guitar case securely set across her lap, wearing that stoic expression of hers that plainly said, *I'd rather be somewhere practicing*. Sara sat next to Maybelle with her right arm draped loosely across a carrying case contoured to the unusual and specific shape of her autoharp within.

The case was a new acquisition, picked up on a recent recording date in Memphis. Sara was quite fond of it. Its hard-shell casing protected her autoharp from water, dust and humidity, any of which could affect the instrument's performance. A convenient flip-top compartment stored her tuning wrench and picks. The precious instrument within, cradled in soft green felt, was an old favorite. The 8-chord Model 72 8/8s autoharp was Sara's prize possession.

New York, thought Sara. Things to do. Fame. Money. But with eyelids growing heavier by the minute, oblivious to the hustling and bustling around her, she found her mind drifting, in a sort of half-sleep, back to their Clinch Mountain home in Tennessee. She was sitting on the front porch swing. She could hear the trilling of birdsong and smell the morning breeze fragrant with the scent of pine.

That's when she felt the vague breeze brush her shoulder ever so faintly where no breeze had a right to be, there in a crowded hotel lobby. Another heartbeat, and she stirred. The hard-shell carrying case was no longer beneath her arm! The "breeze" had been someone rushing close by her, snagging the case on their way past. Her autoharp was gone! Another heartbeat snapped her wide awake.

She sprang to her feet.

AP had reached the front of the line signing in at the front desk, his back to the lobby, oblivious to what was happening. Maybelle's startled reaction indicated her dawning awareness, but like everyone else, she seemed to Sara to be reacting in slow motion.

And there he was!

A teenager wearing a leather jacket, making a full-speed dash for the hotel lobby's main front entrance. The carrying case was gripped firmly in his left hand, swinging like a mad pendulum at his side as he ran. He didn't wait for a path to clear, using his free elbow and momentum to roughly shove aside unsuspecting people who stood in his path. He flung a glance back over his shoulder without slowing, a sneering, pockmarked snarl of triumph.

The hole he'd made, plunging through the crowd, closed up right behind him, the density of people forming a human wall before Sara could take a single step in pursuit. A few seconds more and he'd be out through those revolving glass doors, onto the Manhattan sidewalk fronting the hotel. He would vanish forever along with her autoharp. What could she do? She could never catch up to the thief in time.

There remained only one thing to do, and so she did it, raising a straight arm to point after the young man who was now less than twenty feet from getting outside. At the top of her voice, Sara shouted.

"Stop, thief!"

CHAPTER TWO

A TALL MAN, sharply dressed, wearing a fedora, seemed to materialize out of the general hubbub of the lobby.

He and a pair of similarly well-turned-out men were just emerging from a cigar shop situated between the street entrance and the front desk. Striding several paces ahead of the others, this tall fellow was in the process of lighting a cigar when Sara's cry pierced the air. The fellow shook out his match, pocketed the unlit cigar and spent a few seconds sizing up the situation. Then he stepped forward, stretching out one of his long legs.

The thief never saw the ankle extended before him.

When his ankle connected with that of the man, the thief lost his balance. His running momentum worked against him, sending the young man sailing airborne for several seconds. This gave bystanders enough time to draw away before he hit the marble floor, sliding across it.

Sara started to force her way through the crowd, making an effort to be polite. She saw the tall man stalk across to where the leather-jacketed lad was regaining his balance. The kid was halfway to his feet. He whirled angrily to face the man who had tripped him, his belligerent sneer now snarling rage. He retained a firm grip on the autoharp's carrying case.

Then he froze when he beheld the face of the man who towered over him. His rage disappeared. His features grew slack. His jaw dropped.

The man said, "You know who I am, boy."

A statement, not a question. An icy, flat voice.

Sara reached the scene through the density of onlookers. The pair of men, with whom the tall fellow had emerged from the cigar store, now stood behind him, the fingertips of the right hand of each man held inches from the lapels of his suit. A hush had fallen over the face-off, a collective holding of breath.

The kid in the leather jacket said in a small, quiet voice, "I—I know who you are."

"That's good." To Sara's surprise, the tall fellow's response was mild, conversational. He indicated Sara with a nod. "I want you to hand that case back to its rightful owner."

The teenager did not hesitate. He did move carefully, his every step precise and cautious. He crossed to stand before Sara. He handed her the carrying case, averting his eyes from hers. Up close Sara could see the beads of sweat that glistened across his pale forehead. He started to turn away.

The tall man wearing the fedora said, "Not so fast."

The kid froze as if a switch had turned off his willpower. He eyed the man with expectant apprehension, saying nothing.

The man said, "Apologize to the lady. You caused her extreme distress and inconvenience."

The boy's Adam's apple bobbed with an audible gulp. Again he obeyed without hesitation, returning to face Sara, still managing to avoid eye contact with her.

"Uh, I'm sorry, ma'am. I been hungry. I know I done wrong. I'm real sorry."

The words poured out, a breathy rush sounding like one long word spoken in a foreign tongue. That said, the young fellow's attention shifted back to the tall man. Expectant. Apprehensive.

The man said, "Okay, punk. Scram. Don't let me catch you round here again, got me?"

"Yes, sir. Gotcha!"

Sara didn't hear any fake sincerity.

The would-be thief spun on his heel and was gone, dashing out into the street, vanishing from sight. The normal activity of the lobby resumed. The two companions, whose fingertips had so indiscreetly hovered near their lapels, relaxed visibly now that the confrontation was past.

Sara could not take her eyes from the commanding figure and presence of the tall man in the fedora. A single shaft of sunlight seemed to catch him like a spotlight, though she knew that had to be an illusion. But his physical appearance was no illusion. A well-muscled build topped with a thatch of wavy blond hair. A snappy dresser. She judged, placing him in his 20s, though life had seasoned him much. She could tell that at a glance without knowing a thing about him.

Then he was sauntering toward her!

Sara's breath caught in her throat. She held the autoharp case to her with both arms, like a schoolgirl would hold her books. Her anxiety had faded from just knowing she had her beloved instrument back again. The autoharp meant the world to her. She couldn't imagine her life without it. It wasn't only about performing for others. There were also those private moments alone when the autoharp's lovely sounds comforted and nurtured her, giving her the strength to push on. She'd almost lost all of that but for the actions of this handsome city fellow who now stood squarely before her.

He said, "I hope it wasn't damaged, whatever it is."

"It's an autoharp," Sara heard herself say.

He smiled with toothy warmth.

"A what?"

His presence had her flustered. Not a condition Sara was used to. No matter what she might be feeling or thinking, Sara Carter always appeared composed. A woman careful with her words. Not this time.

"It's a musical instrument I play. I'm the musician." She heard herself prattle on like a schoolgirl. "My name is Sara," and she extended her hand around the carrying case.

They shook hands. His grip was pleasant enough although his flesh was cool to her touch.

He said, "Nice to meet you, Sara. I'm Vincent."

Sara thought, *what a nice name for this nice young man...*

She said, "Thank you so much for stepping in. My autoharp is quite valuable...to me especially, I mean."

He regarded the formidable hard-shell case.

"I can see that."

"You certainly did a wonderful job of handling that miscreant. I truly am most grateful. Are you the house detective?"

That brought a mild chuckle.

"No, ma'am." His right thumb and index finger touched the brim of his fedora in a gentlemanly gesture. "Just a private citizen doing his good deed for the day."

"Well you certainly did that. Thank you, Vincent."

With that she started to turn away, to rejoin Maybelle.

Vincent said, "Sara, how about a cup of coffee? Or," he nodded toward the nearest tea room, "if you'd prefer a drink..."

Sara thought, *and in addition to everything else, he surely is a brash fellow!*

Along with her rural appearance and southern accent, he surely had not missed the wedding ring on her left hand. Her relationship to AP was in name only after the torrid events of the preceding summer. Still...

She sent him the hint of a small smile, flirting but only mildly.

"City men certainly do move fast."

"Only when they have to," said Vincent. "This is a hotel. People come and are gone before you know it. Well, what do you say?"

Sara forced herself to remember who and where she was. The Carter Family group was booked and known as a family. Appearances had to be kept up.

"That's a powerful fine offer, Vincent, but I must refuse, and you know why." She held up her left hand so he could not possibly miss seeing her wedding ring.

"Just not my day, I guess," Vincent said with an amiable sigh.

Sara added, "And I do need to be on my way. Thank you again. It's been so nice meeting you."

With that, there seemed nothing more to say. She withdrew. She did pause briefly after a few steps to send a passing glance after Vincent and his two friends. She was thinking that a warm smile and a cool touch made for an interesting combination in a man.

As they made their way through the lobby toward the street entrance, the three men were chuckling heartily among themselves as if one of them had said something amusing. Then they were out on the street and gone.

By the time Sara reached Maybelle, less than two minutes had elapsed since the would-be thief had made his move. Maybelle had always been the practical one. She had remained standing by their luggage. But she had observed from there.

"Dang if that wasn't something."

Sara rested the carrying case on the cushiony sofa,

keeping a strong grip this time on its handle. She was surprised to realize she was out of breath.

"You saw?"

"Saw it all. Who was that good-looking feller who came to your rescue?"

"His name is Vincent. Maybelle, he asked me for coffee. He asked me if I wanted to go for a drink."

"A drink? Dang. That would sure enough raise eyebrows back home, now wouldn't it?"

"I reckon. I told him no, of course. I'm a married woman, Maybelle. He had to have seen my ring. But he asked anyway."

"They move fast in New York, that's for sure"

"That's what I told him."

"If it ain't nailed down," said Maybelle, "some rascal will snag it sure enough be it man, woman or property." She gave a small laugh. "Not too different from back in the hills, I reckon."

"But he was something, wasn't he," said Sara, "the way he stepped right in and took charge like he did. Like the white knight coming to my rescue."

Maybelle rolled her eyes.

"Oh, brother. Girl, are you forgetting what happened last summer?"

"Of course not. How could I forget? But—"

"Hush now," said Maybelle. "Here comes AP."

CHAPTER THREE

"WHERE THE DEVIL IS JIMMIE RODGERS?"

At age 40, Ralph Peer was dynamic and urban. A well-groomed man who exuded in his every manner, word, and deed the energy of one supremely self-confident, aglow with a patina of intellectual sophistication. He was not happy as he surveyed the three people seated before him in his hotel suite. His tone, not impolite, did compel a reply. Rodgers, who was booked to costar with the Carter Family in tonight's concert at Carnegie Hall, had yet to put in an appearance.

Sara and Maybelle fidgeted uncomfortably, turning to AP, who maintained a stoic countenance. Peer had long ago learned that AP rarely spoke or smiled unless he had to and then with never a wasted word.

AP spoke after enough time had elapsed with no one answering.

"Shoot, Mr. Peer, I don't reckon it would be any great loss if that rounder, Jimmie Rodgers, didn't show up at all."

Maybelle said, rather gently, "Now AP, them records we made last year with Jimmie turned out just fine. He just wasn't having a good day last time we seen him, is all."

AP said, "He flirted with you, Maybelle, last time we seen him! We all seen it, and you being a married woman."

Sara said, "Now, AP."

Her softly spoken rebuke made Peer think of a punch delivered inside a velvet glove.

While Peer hadn't been present at the session they were referring to the previous year, everything that happened on that date, or at any other Peer-produced recording session, did eventually make its way back to the main office in New York.

Peer said, "Maybelle, you made a valuable contribution to that session. Jimmie was under the weather with that blasted TB. Too weak to play his guitar so you covered for him on a couple songs, playing his part so he could concentrate on his singing. You saved that day."

Maybelle said, "Pshaw."

AP persisted.

"Point is, Mr. Peer, that feller's music ain't nothing like ours in the first place. You know that's so. Raising sand. Wild times. Whiskey and fornication. Gunplay. We don't stand for none of that ungodly mess."

Peer said, with as much patience as he could muster, "AP, I believe you're missing the point here. You're missing what I'm trying to do with this concert tonight. Being at Carnegie Hall, this show is going to generate a lot of attention in the newspapers and on the radio. Anyone with even a little interest in music is going to know about it. My idea is to put your music out to a wider audience than we already have. And that includes folks who are fans of Jimmie Rodgers. That's what tonight is really about. Increasing our revenue by expanding our audience."

"Well," AP conceded with a drawn out sigh, "reckon there ain't nothing wrong with that."

"Most certainly not," said Peer. Relieved that the often obstinate AP was listening to reason, he seized the moment to elaborate. "Your folks' music and Jimmie's is like the two sides of life, don't you see? The Carter Family has those high ideals in your music. But there's no denying the other side of life that Jimmie sings about. That's what people love about what they're starting to call country music. Between Jimmie and you Carters, this Carnegie Hall show will present everything this new music is about."

Peer had learned the business of making records and selling music from the ground up, starting twenty years earlier as a clerk in the Victor Records credit department. That position didn't last long. He cut a deal whereby he agreed to work without salary on the condition that he receive a cut of the royalties for every record sold and every song played on the radio, thus earning him one million dollars a year.

So where the hell was Jimmie Rodgers?

From past experience, Peer had a good idea. He quite liked the rough and rowdy "Singing Brakeman," but well knew how susceptible Jimmie was to the lures of wayward women and high times, both of which were always in plentiful supply in New York. He could only assure himself that Jimmie *would* show up...

The Carter Family, on the other hand, had never missed a show, although this time around, Peer could not help but notice a chilly distance that seemed to exist between Sara and AP. Never an overly affectionate couple from what Peer could see, on this trip Sara appeared aloof and moody.

The biggest reason Peer signed the group was the unmistakable voice of Sara Carter, a not unattractive mountain woman when he first made her acquaintance in Bristol and a short time later when he visited the Carters in Tennessee. But these days, she had certainly "cleaned up good" as the mountainfolk would say. A stylish black dress with a smart white belt accentuated her attractive figure.

While her intonation and lyrics on record were traditional, you could hear on the recordings who she was—a modern woman in many ways. There was obviously some sort of pressure on Sara and AP's marriage, but the public must know nothing about it. Peer had done his best to impress upon them that it was important their audience not be aware of any domestic difficulty. The Carter Family was, after all, being promoted as representing and appealing to domestic values. Maybelle and AP generally treated Sara with deference. Maybelle, nearly always dead serious about everything, especially her guitar playing, seemed to be the only person Sara truly confided in. With everyone else Sara was aloof, accommodating yet distant.

The honest truth was that as a recording act, Sara and Maybelle could have done just fine as a duo. AP's contributions to the Carter Family's recording sessions were minimal. Some guitar. Some harmony. AP was not even present at the second of those sessions in Bristol. He was off buying a tire since one had gone flat and been crudely patched on the drive to Bristol. And yet the Carter Family without AP Carter was unthinkable. He was the genius behind it all, the one who acquired the countless old traditional songs that comprised their vast repertoire. AP and Maybelle then arranged the songs, and Sara sang them. But it was AP who'd been instrumental in putting their group together in the first place and bringing the Carter Family to Ralph Peer's attention.

Maybelle cleared her throat.

"May I ask what order we'll be performing in?"

Peer smiled expansively.

"You certainly may ask anything you wish, Maybelle. That's why we're having this meeting and why I wish Jimmie were here with us now. He's going to open the show. He'll lift the rafters with those good timing songs and his personality. He'll get that New York crowd on their feet hooting and hollering no matter how sophisticated they think they are.

Then you folks will come on. You'll provide balm for their ears and soul. Yes sir, it will be quite a package, yes sir. Too much planning and effort, not to mention money, has been invested in this concert for it to not go on *exactly* as I have it planned."

A loud, full-throated hillbilly yodel suddenly pierced the air.

Startled, everyone in the suite brought their eyes around in the direction of the archway of the short hallway to the front door. There in the archway, in all his hubris and *joie di vivre*, stood The Singing Brakeman, The Blue Yodeler his own self. Jimmie Rodgers wore a white linen suit and a white, wide-brimmed cowboy hat. Cowboy boots firmly planted, hands on his hips, a wide smile across his friendly face.

Peer had always enjoyed the fellow's company. Jimmie Rodgers was a grand showman. The genuine article. Always amusing company, Jimmie was a gifted and prolific songwriter. During the past few years, as his manager and agent, Peer had recorded and marketed more than one hundred Rodgers compositions. Every one of them sold well.

Few among Jimmie's adoring multitude of fans were aware that his boisterous talent and good timing attitude were in fact the carefully maintained façade of a very sick man. This endeared him more than anything to Ralph Peer on a man-to-man level, the way Jimmie persevered despite the ravages to his body wrought by tuberculosis. Seen up close, Jimmie's color was ashen. He looked at least twenty years past his true age of thirty-four. And yet his irrepressible personality always shone brightly.

Peer crossed over to shake hands with the new arrival, warmly clasping Rodgers's shoulder.

"Welcome, Jimmie! I knew you wouldn't let us down."

"Door wasn't locked," said Jimmie. "Figured I was expected so I just waltzed my way in."

"Of course, Jimmie, of course. Good to see you. We've been waiting for you."

Jimmie's eyes panned the Carters with a dour gaze. He passed over Sara and Maybelle to settle on AP.

"Yeah, I heard." He said to AP, "Don't worry, old-timer. You folks are topping the bill. Heck, it's only show business. Ain't that right, Mr. Peer?"

AP's stoic demeanor revealed no reaction. He said nothing.

"That's exactly right, Jimmie," said Peer. He turned to take in the others in a manner warming now that the final piece of his puzzle—Jimmie—was in place. "This Carnegie Hall country concert will be an important professional turning point for all of us. My friends, we're on a grand adventure, and we will not fail!"

Jimmie said, "Darn tootin'. Why, folks, we're about to show New York what downhome is all about, ain't that right?"

With little sign of life, AP intoned, "I reckon."

Maybelle smiled. "It's good to see you again, Jimmie. I'll be there to fill in behind you on guitar if need be."

"Bless your heart, darlin'," said Jimmie, "and thank you kindly. But I'm feeling all right these days, I'm glad to say. Fit as a fiddle for the big show."

Sara said, "That's good to hear, Jimmie."

"Damned TB," Jimmie went on, "comes and goes like a thief in the gol-durn night. One day feels like I'm ready for 'em to start shoveling dirt in my face. Next day I'm up and ready for some serious honky-tonkin'. Shucks, woke up this morning feeling downright frisky!" He doffed his hat, bowing in a courtly fashion. "Good to see you again, Sara."

Sara lowered her eyes demurely.

"Jimmie."

Observing this, Peer found it a bit much but kept his thoughts to himself. The cheeky fellow was now practically flirting with a married woman right in front of her husband! Peer told himself he must keep an eye on any situation. He would have words with Jimmie in private. What a character the fellow was!

To stay on track and keep everyone's spirits up, Peer enthused, "Yes sir, it will be quite a show. Music representing the two sides of life, yes sir. Some day in the future people around the world will be listening to the music you folks are playing.

"Dang right," said Jimmie.

"Pshaw," said Sara.

"We'll be in our graves by then," Peer conceded, "but it will happen, I guarantee. Musicians in the future will take your music and will come up with music we can't imagine."

Maybelle said, "Mr. Peer, are you joshing us?"

"Not a bit of it," said Peer. "Blues and country music is just the beginning."

"Yep," said Jimmie, "one big happy family, that's us! Right, folks? One for all, and all for one! That's the ticket. They say this here Big ol' Apple is a dangerous place. But any of these gangster fellers decide to mess with us, they'll learn right quick that another handle for me out West is Pistol Packing Pappy."

He held aside the lapel of his jacket with the fingers of his left hand. His right hand unholstered a silver automatic pistol with a fancy pearl grip. He tossed the gun from hand to hand a couple of times, a well-executed "border shift," before spinning the gun three times around his index finger before returning the piece to its holster, allowing his lapel to fall back into place, concealing the weapon.

Maybelle's eyes brightened with amusement.

"Jimmie, you devil! You wouldn't use that gun on anybody, would you? You're just joshing, trying to scare us."

With a glint in his eye, Jimmie patted the concealed pistol through his jacket.

He said, "Am I?"

Ralph Peer did not like the sound of that.

Too much could go haywire with this gaggle of hillbillies loose in his big town. He'd have to stay on his toes and not leave anything to chance. Between talk like Jimmie's and the tension he sensed now existing between AP and Sara, trouble was just waiting to happen.

CHAPTER FOUR

ON THIS TRIP to New York, the accommodations provided for the Carter Family were, to Maybelle's way of thinking, a vast improvement. She and Sara shared an elegantly furnished room—two plush beds, a bath, and plenty of closet space. AP and Jimmie Rodgers shared a similar room across the hall. Mr. Peer's suite was several floors above.

In their room, Sara lay atop her bed, sulking.

Maybelle sat on the edge of her bed, strumming her guitar, working on the accompaniment she had in mind for one of AP's new songs. They'd started working on the number before leaving Tennessee. Maybelle considered herself a perfectionist in most things, especially when it came to guitar playing. There were few things in the world that meant as much to Maybelle as her guitar and the sounds she worked to coax from it. Her mother had raised ten children. Maybelle's father was proprietor of a general store. There wasn't much money around, but there was plenty of music in them mountains. You played for each other, for the frolics when the chores were done on Saturday night. A lot of people made their own instruments. Her brothers had given her a guitar, and by the time she was twelve, Maybelle was winning regional picking contests, learning ballads such as *Wildwood Flower* from her mother, who learned them from her mother before her, who had in turn learned them from her parents.

Back home, after the house quieted down and the chores were done, that's when they'd make music. Maybelle harmonizing with Sara's rich alto. Sara strumming her autoharp. Maybelle perfecting a unique guitar style, playing rhythm and the tune at the same time, picking out the melody on the bass string with her thumb while brushing the chords on the high strings. They were cousins, Maybelle and Sara, who'd grown up living about a mile apart and had become sisters-in-law. They'd grown closer and closer over the years, until now when the two of them almost thought as one.

No, thought Maybelle, that wasn't quite right. She and Sara knew each other's life intimately, yes, but they remained two very different personalities. Sara was several years Maybelle's senior, but beyond that, they were much alike but with some differences. Sara was a dreamer. An emotional, romantic free spirit. And Maybelle, the disciplined one, always, it seemed, with her nose to the grindstone. The cousins cared for and about each other with the depth of feeling of twin sisters. But they were not alike.

The Waldorf offered accommodations Maybelle would never have dreamed of a few short years ago. In their early days of performing, the Carter Family played most often for church and at community gatherings—day trips, bedding down for the night with family or friends in their homes. Then, once the records began selling, widening their performance circuit, they would often stay in boarding houses boasting indoor plumbing that had seemed, in those days, like the height of luxurious living.

A preliminary visit to Carnegie Hall was scheduled for that afternoon. After announcing this, Mr. Peer had invited everyone to join him in the Waldorf's sumptuous dining room for a breakfast buffet. Jimmie had readily accepted while the Carters declined and politely withdrew. They'd imbibed a large breakfast in the dining car before their train's arrival in New York. At present, AP was ensconced alone in his room across the hall.

Maybelle paused in her guitar playing.

"You know what we need, kid? We need us some fresh air. Let's head out and spend some time this morning on our own."

"All them city gals," said Sara, as if speaking to the ceiling, "I bet they don't have some man telling them what they can and can't do every hour of the durn day."

Maybelle replaced her guitar in its case.

"I wouldn't be too sure about that." She gestured to indicate their surroundings. "Far as this girl's concerned, this beats heck out of milking cows."

Sara emitted a weary sigh.

"Does it? I don't know, Maybelle. Part of me wants to quit all this straight up and follow Coy out to California."

Hearing this, Maybelle tightened up inside.

"Honey, you've got to stop thinking about that man. You and AP have three young 'uns at home. What about your children? What about them?"

"I'm talking about leaving Tennessee," said Sara, "not disappearing off the face of the earth. I'd be sure 'nuff coming back for regular for visits, and Lord knows my kids have plenty of extended family down home to look after 'em and see they're raised right. Don't you reckon that'd be better for 'em growing up than to have Mama always pining away for someone else so deep in her heart who ain't around?"

"And what about AP?" pressed Maybelle. "That man's doing his best in his way to move on after what happened last summer."

"Doing his best." Sara repeated the words with another sigh. "AP should have been doing his best last winter instead of taking off. Me and the children had to make it on our own without him even leaving us firewood or provisions. No, not that worthless husband of mine. Always living in his own world and nothing else. Sometimes it's like the real world don't even matter to him except for his music. Had to go traipsing off, saying he needed to find us songs. Songs don't keep a body warm on a cold night on the mountain. If AP had stayed at home to provide for his family, I woulda never met his cousin Coy in the first place. Doing his best," she said again and gave an unladylike snort at the ceiling.

"Sara, he's your husband. AP loves you deeply."

Sara turned her head on the pillow to make eye contact with Maybelle.

"After Coy, that ain't enough."

"Aw come on, girl. This ain't the time for talk like that. With us playing Carnegie Hall, you're not thinking 'bout breaking up the act, are you?"

Sara cracked smile. The moment passed.

"I reckon not. I am sorry, Maybelle. I'm doing the best I can too."

Maybelle knew all about Coy Bays. Yes, indeed. Coy and Sara's torrid relationship was still fresh in everyone's mind, having ended only months earlier.

The strain on AP and Sara's marriage was naturally catastrophic. Coy was AP's cousin who stepped in to help Sara out with the farm chores when AP had taken off to go song-hunting, leaving Sara and the kids alone. One thing had led to another, nature taking its course with Coy and Sara given the circumstance they found themselves in. Their affair became the talk of the valley, ending only after the entire Bays family—Coy, his parents and siblings—up and moved not only out of the valley, but all the way out to California.

The emotional scars between Sara and AP remained, not

yet healed. There'd always been a sort of natural distance maintained between AP and Sara. Neither of them ever showed affection for the other in public. Maybelle was country, but she knew human nature was universal. Some scars never heal. And so Sara and AP persevered—at home, in the studio, and performing on the road. They could ill afford at this point, in the depths of a global depression, to break up the Carter Family.

The show must go on.

Both on the road and back home in Tennessee, Maybelle had fallen into the role of running interference between Sara and AP, not always an easy task. The occasional domestic spat would flare up between them without warning. You never knew when or where or what might trigger it. The frigid distance between Sara and AP was palpable, likely even to a stranger and certainly to someone as perceptive as Mr. Peer. For the most part, though, the three of them were doing their best to make the situation work.

An incident like what happened in the lobby, the attempted theft of Sara's autoharp, might easily have escalated into AP criticizing Sara for not being more careful. But AP had been at front desk, busy with signing them in. It wasn't until after the dapper fellow, Vincent, and his friends had left the lobby that AP had finally showed up with a bellhop who helped with the luggage and showed them to their rooms. AP tipped the boy frugally and had said nothing about the lobby incident. He certainly would have, thought Maybelle, had he witnessed it.

Maybelle knew her cousin/sister-in-law/best friend well enough to know what had triggered Sara's current moodiness. Vincent. The "white knight" who'd retrieved her autoharp. Had they seen the last of Vincent? Maybelle resolved to nip in the bud the potential trouble she could see along those lines.

She clamped shut the metal clasps of her guitar case, then crossed over to sit on the edge of Sara's bed.

"Uh, honey, there is something I've been wanting to say about that fellow in the lobby. This is the first chance I've had."

"Vincent?"

"Yes, Vincent. Sara, when he stepped in to stop that thief—"

"You mean when he came to my rescue."

"Okay, when he came to your rescue. Did you happen to notice those two friends he was with?"

"No, not really. Why?"

"Well, when Vincent stepped in to tangle with that feller who had your autoharp, there was a few seconds when no one knew what was going to happen next."

"I know. It was exciting, wasn't it? Maybelle, I was there. What about his friends?"

"Well, them friends, they stood there reaching under their jackets while your friend Vincent took that boy down."

"So? And knock off the friend business about Vincent, if you don't mind. I'll never see the man again. He was a gallant gentleman who did me a kind turn. End of story."

"Sara, they were reaching for guns. They looked just the way gangsters look in the movies when they reach for their guns."

"Did you see any guns?"

"Well, no."

Sara chuckled. She propped herself on an elbow, no longer moody.

"You've seen too many gangster movies, and if your right about them carrying guns, so what? What if they were his bodyguards?"

"Bodyguards?"

"The big city means big money, Maybelle. A lot of rich people have bodyguards in these parts. I'll bet Vincent and his friends are businessmen. We're talking high cotton investors or some such. You saw what sharp dressers they were."

Maybelle knew when she was beat. It would be nice if Sara wasn't so flighty and emotional, but at least Sara's emotions were genuine and ran deep. And as her best friend, what could Maybelle do but commiserate?

"Forget it," Maybelle said. "Let's go shopping."

CHAPTER FIVE

ARNOLD FRATELLI WAS BEGGING for his life.

He struggled in vain against the knotted length of rope that bound him to a wooden kitchen chair. He was breathing heavily. Balding and overweight, his pudgy face was flushed a bright red with pearls of sweat big as raindrops.

"Vince, tell me you're not gonna do this thing! We're pals, right? Me and you, we've been on some good capers, ain't we? You can't kill me!"

"Yes, I can," said Vince. He sat on a bench a few feet away, methodically reassembling a .38 caliber revolver that he'd just cleaned and oiled. "Those good time capers you're talking about were before you signed up with the Dutchman."

They were in a lighted corner of an otherwise dark, dingy, unused warehouse. The damp cold of winter permeated the high-ceilinged interior. A faucet drip-dripped somewhere nearby, the sound practically inaudible beneath Fratelli's heavy breathing.

Trigger stood leaning idly against a nearby wall. Trigger's real name was Wilbur. He was only nineteen with a sour disposition and flaming acne. A brace of .45 automatics rode in shoulder leather under each skinny arm. Trigger wasn't much to look at, and it seemed as if the weight of those heavy pistols might topple him over if he wasn't careful. But he was fast on the draw and accurate on the trigger, so Vince kept him around. He'd personally seen the kid shoot down men on three separate occasions, one time for simply laughing when he heard the kid's real name. Trigger had already carved eleven notches into the grip of one of his .45s.

Fratelli started crying. Real tears rolled down his cheeks from both eyes.

"But jeez, Vince, after all we've been through together." He was gasping for breath. "Don't do it! *Please don't do it!*"

"Aw, quit your sniveling," said Vince. "You don't mean nothing to me, you toad. Dutch, he killed my brother and a whole mess of my boys just because I cut myself in for a piece of his action. My brother, Arnie. Dutch Schultz killed my brother. Have you got a brother, Arn?"

Fratelli's Adam's apple bobbed uncontrollably.

"No, Vince," he muttered. "I ain't got no brother."

"Well, neither do I. Not anymore. Not after your boss Dutch had Petey wiped out with a Thompson submachine gun. It was like a part of me died."

"Aw, Vince, please! I'm sorry about your brother. But I didn't have nothing to do with that, I swear. I just keep the books for Dutch, you know that." The words came out in a rushed panic. "It ain't just me. It's Shirley and the kids. What about them? How will they make it without me? I don't wanna die, Vince! There's got to be some way we can work this out."

Setting the pistol aside, Vince turned with what seemed a reasonable, sympathetic expression.

"Now, Arn, you know it's not up to me. Dutch received my ransom demand. It's in his hands now, whether he pays up to get you back, or you stop breathing." He gave a soft, fleshy double palm pat to the side of Fratelli's face. "I'm sure

Dutch will come through for you. Really, Arn, you don't have a thing to worry about."

Fratelli nodded frantically, wanting desperately to believe.

"Yeah, I know, Vince. You're right, I know that. The Dutchman, he'll pay off to get me back. You wait and see. But, Vince, what if he don't? I'm begging you. Please dear God, don't kill me. I'll leave town. I'll leave the rackets. I'll do anything you want, Vince. I don't want to die."

Vince chuckled. "I can see that." He returned to reassembling the .38, snapping in the cylinder with a flick of his wrist and giving it a spin.

The street door behind them opened.

Trigger whirled, both of his .45s seeming to leap into his hands. He holstered the guns when the clicking of high heels brought in Lottie Kreisberger.

Lottie was an extremely well-preserved thirty-two, a brunette with flashing blue eyes, delicate cheekbones and porcelain pale skin. Always stylishly-dressed, Lottie carried herself with a self-confidence most considered aggressive and brassy in a woman. Not that Lottie gave much of a good goddamn about what people thought. She was tough and beautiful, and she knew it.

Some called her Vince Coll's moll. But she was more than that. Much more. It had been Lottie's idea to start kidnapping other gangsters and hold them for ransom, which effectively cut the police out of the picture, since under no circumstance did criminals ever resort to the authorities over such a matter. This was the third time they'd pulled such a caper. Fratelli was the first of Dutch's men they'd snatched. He was Dutch's bookkeeper, a key figure in Schultz's organization

Lottie was carrying a brown paper grocer's sack. With a triumphant smile she set the sack on the bench before Vince.

She said, "Payday."

Vince reached into the bulging paper sack. He withdrew a handful of hundred-dollar bills. Smiling his satisfaction, he peered into the sack full of the money.

"Any trouble?"

Lottie shook her head, no.

"They sent a ten-year-old kid. He showed up on the street corner with the payoff just like they told him to. I counted it in the taxi on the way over here. It's all there. Ten grand."

Vince turned to the man tied to the chair.

"Well, Arnie, looks like the Dutchman stepped in to save your worthless butt."

Fratelli's relief was visible. He stopped struggling against his bonds.

"I knew Dutch would come through. Thank God! I sure didn't want to die."

Vince said, "Untie him, Trigger."

Trigger went about doing so.

The words were now flowing out of Fratelli. His eyes remained wary like a man regarding a rattlesnake, cautious of what it may do next.

"Vince, I want you to know there's no hard feelings far as you and me go, okay? I understand what you done was business because you've got it in for Dutch. I just got caught in the middle, right? But for you and Lottie here, it was just business so I want you to know, no hard feelings. Right?"

Vince warmly assured him, "Of course, Arn, of course. Like you said, it's just business. Ain't that right, Lottie?"

Lottie nodded, coldly eyeing the disheveled Fratelli.

She said, "That's right, Arnie. We've got nothing against you personally like Vince said."

Vince added, "But there is one last thing."

Fratelli sank back onto the chair, suddenly apprehensive.

"What's that?"

Vince picked up the revolver he'd been cleaning.

He said, "We're going to play a little game before you leave."

"Game?"

"It's called Russian roulette. Ever hear of it?"

Fratelli's florid complexion went pasty white.

He said, "Vince, no..."

Vince held out the .38, grip first, holding the gun by the barrel.

"Take it, Arnie, old pal."

"No, Vince. Please. Dutch paid you off! You gotta let me go!"

"Take the gun, Arnie. Spin the cylinder. There's one bullet in a chamber. That makes it only one chance out of six of you losing. Do it, Arn, or I'll have Trigger put one into the back of your head, and there's no damn chance of you surviving if you won't play."

"Vince, please, I'm beggin' ya. Don't make me do this!"

"Do it."

Fratelli's frightened eyes swept to Lottie as if considering pleading with her to intervene. But Lottie stood there lighting a cigarette, regarding the unfolding drama with a neutral detachment.

Realizing there was no choice, no hope, a tremor began shuddering through Arn Fratelli. He raised the pistol to his right temple in an impulsive surge.

"Damn you to hell, Vince Coll," he said.

He pulled the trigger.

The gun blast was magnified by the confines of the warehouse. The overweight Fratelli and his chair pitched sideways to the floor, an ugly reddish-gray mural of blood, brains, and bone chips splashing across the wall. A blueish gray haze of gun smoke lingered in the air.

Vince pried the pistol loose from Fratelli's dead fingers. He gave the cylinder a spin.

"Doggone it," he said. "Guess I made a mistake. Forgot

I'd loaded the damn piece full-up! Seeing all that money, guess it made me sort of forget."

Lottie eyed him, detached and cool. She knew her man. Vincent could assume a slick, charming manner, when inclined or called upon to do so, that could charm a nun out of her knickers. But the truth? He was a brutal savage without a conscience, a leader of hardened criminals capable of any act of force or deception that suited him.

She didn't bother looking at the corpse.

She said, "Was that smart, lover? Could make it tough drumming up future payoffs if they know you're going to smoke the guy anyway."

Vince slipped the .38 under his jacket, into a concealed shoulder holster.

"Couldn't help myself, babe. We'll have enough other ways to generate cash soon enough once I cut that rat Dutch down to size." He regarded Fratelli's remains, now puddling the concrete floor with blood. "I get a kick out of seeing people die, I really do. Ain't it something the way one second they're palpitatin' all over the place, begging for mercy and all of that. Two seconds later they're nothing but a mess of dead blubber taking up space. I like the way they beg me not to do it. I wonder where they go after I kill 'em."

Lottie said, "You'll find out soon enough."

"What's that supposed to mean?"

Vince's response was a defensive challenge. Lottie defused the moment with a long draw on her cigarette and a dismissive shrug.

"Nobody lives forever. What's done is done. What's next?"

Vince handed her the bulging grocery sack.

"Here, stash this the usual way." With a nod he indicated Fratelli's corpse. "Have Trigger and the boys dump the stiff."

Trigger assured him, "Don't worry about a thing, boss."

"I never do," said Vince.

Lottie said, "And where are you off to?"

Vince used an index finger to smooth down the brim of his fedora.

"I just remembered an appointment."

And then he was out the door.

CHAPTER SIX

SARA AND MAYBELLE returned to the Waldorf weighed down with packages acquired during their shopping spree, each having purchased a new pair of shoes, a new hat, frocks, accessories, and unmentionables. The new hat boxes were particularly cumbersome, resulting in a challenging journey from their taxicab, forging their way through the Waldorf's busy lobby.

Sara said with a chuckle, "Reckon it's just as well we only made it to two stores."

Her state of mind had improved, which did not stop herself from thinking about Coy Bays. An afternoon of big city clothes shopping with Maybelle was not enough to stop her from thinking about the man she still loved. Months had gone by. Their affair was over. She knew that. But she could not get Coy, and what they'd shared the summer before, out of her mind. Would he have liked the hat she bought and the new scarf to go with it? Coy would never see these things living with his family in California.

No one understood her the way Coy did, and that included Maybelle and AP, the man she'd married so many years ago. No other woman she could think of was living a life like her and Maybelle. Women in the hills of Tennessee stayed home and had babies. They cooked, cleaned, and raised a garden. They didn't have careers. Even as the Carter Family became popular and began touring, Sara and Maybelle still continued their normal country life—weeding, milking cows, slopping hogs, gathering eggs, canning vegetable, churning butter, washing clothes on a board, preparing meals...all of the chores required to maintain a small farm. Once the work was done, then they cleaned up, put on their Sunday best and got on the road playing engagements, leaving the children with Grandma Carter.

The life of a recording, traveling musician did not bring Sara the same satisfaction it brought Maybelle and AP. The money was good. Yes, it was nice having warmth in the winter, indoor plumbing, food on the table, and even a modest nest egg in the bank. There was the inner satisfaction when the music was spot-on and those fun times like today's shopping trip. Still, her singing voice, Maybelle's guitar playing, and AP's songs had created a life for her that she could only accept. Her heart, her soul, would always be in Clinch Mountain, a way of life so hard while at the same time so nurturing and complete unto itself. Yet she'd been an unfaithful wife. In that Clinch Mountain world she so loved, she would forever be a branded woman.

As for Coy, who was she kidding? Likely she would never see him again. That was certainly the idea behind his entire family relocating to the other side of the country! They had not been in contact since. And yet Coy and the tempestuous, passionate, *too brief* affair they'd shared were never far from Sara's mind.

She and Maybelle were halfway across the Waldorf's crowded lobby, approaching the bank of elevators, when Maybelle drew up short.

She said, "Uh oh."

Sara followed the direction of her gaze.

There was much concentrated activity around the unsynchronized arrival and departure of four elevators, a steady flow of people boarding after passengers from the upper floors had debarked.

A tall man, wearing a snap-brim fedora, stood on the far side of the bank of elevators, apart from the concentrated activity. He stood looking directly at Sara through the crowd of people, notable for two reasons. He was taller than anyone around him, and he seemed to be the only person in the entire Waldorf lobby who was not hurrying to be somewhere else. He stood there like a rooted tree.

Waiting for her?

That had to be the case! They made eye contact. The small smile he wore broke into a toothy grin, wide as his face. He started politely elbowing his way through the crowd.

Sara said, "Maybelle, it's Vincent!"

Maybelle responded without hesitation or enthusiasm.

"I see him."

"This is your chance to meet him. I'll introduce you."

"No thanks. I'll see you up in the room."

Maybelle cut sharply away, wasting no time angling toward an elevator that had practically filled to capacity. She was the last to board. The elevator boy reached across closing the door. Maybelle and her armful of packages and boxes disappeared from view, leaving Sara to stand face to face with the tall man who stood before her.

The wide, toothy grin again became the charming smile.

He said, "Hello again."

Sara felt like her heart was a lump in her throat, and for an instant she feared she'd lost her voice.

Then she managed, "Hello, Vincent. What a coincidence! I hadn't expected to see you again."

"Please call me Vince."

"Okay...Vince."

"Us meeting here like this is no coincidence," he said. "I've been staked out here hoping to catch sight of you."

She heard herself say, "Oh my."

He regarded her assortment of packages and the hat box.

"You've had a busy morning, I see."

That brought a slight self-conscious chuckle from Sara.

"Maybelle and I don't get to the city that often." She didn't know what to say next so she tacked on, "I hope your day is going well."

"I'm having a great day," he said. "Made a killing and settled a score."

"That's wonderful."

He added, "The only way I could make this day better is to spend some time with you."

Sara felt a warm rush and could only hope to dickens that she wasn't blushing!

"Oh, Vincent. Vince. Don't you know I'm a married woman?"

"Doesn't matter," said Vince. "I like you, Sara. I'd like to get to know you better."

Sara said, "Oh, dear."

Vince pointed through the across the busy lobby.

"See that tea room over there?"

"Yes."

"Wouldn't a cup of tea be nice?"

A voice inside her head was shouting, *Sara, don't do it!* She told herself, I'm restless. I'm not crazy! That is, not counting last year. But this fellow is so nice. So good looking! A successful businessman from the city found her attractive and interesting. *And why shouldn't he?* Sara asked herself. I *am* interesting and attractive.

Sure, the inner voice countered, *an attractive, interesting farm girl who traipsed through the land with a husband who never had learned how to treat her and a beloved sister-in-law who wants things to stay just as they are. And now here's Vincent...*

She must rein in these emotions.

"Vince, I'd love to but I simply can't. You must understand."

"Sara—"

"No. I'm sorry. It's not just that I'm a married woman, though I reckon that surely should be enough. But Vince, I have responsibilities to others. Other people count on me. I'm a musician in a group, you see, and we have an appearance scheduled for tonight at Carnegie Hall. A dress rehearsal is scheduled for this afternoon. So you see I couldn't possibly—"

"Tell you what," said Vince. He sounded comfortable speaking with authority. "I'll be sitting at a corner table in that tea room at four o'clock this afternoon. Will you be back from your dress rehearsal by then?"

"I...I suppose so."

"Why don't you join me, Sara? I wish you would."

The invitation stroked Sara's nerve ends, pleasurable as Coy's caress. *No, Sara!* the voice in her head snapped at her.

She heard herself say, "I've told you why I can't see you. Please, Vincent, understand. I'm sorry. I've got to go."

With that she turned with such a blind need to escape that she jostled into someone, almost spilling her packages. She gained the nearest elevator. The boy reached to close its door. Her last view of Vince was him standing there, planted in place amid the bustling crowd.

He was gazing after her, wearing that damnably enticing little smile.

CHAPTER SEVEN

IN THE WINGS of the Carnegie Hall main stage, Jimmie Rodgers stood admiring the way Sara's lovely voice soared out like a bird taking wing across the empty rows of seating. The Carter Family held center stage, performing the closing song of the forty-minute set they had just played to the empty house. The perfect acoustics of the hall caught clearly Sara's pristine delivery accompanied by Maybelle and AP.

The stage, the only lighted area in the vast theater, cloaked the grand hall with an atmosphere of vast shadow, reminding Jimmie of a mountain canyon at dusk.

Ralph Peer stood conversing with a man in the wings on the far side of the stage. There was something familiar about the man. Jimmie couldn't quite place him. Midthirties. Sharp features. Compactly built. His hat was worn cocked at a careless angle. He seemed to be asking pointed questions, prompting Peer to respond at length while the guy made notations in a small notebook. Reporter, thought Jimmie.

The Carters were closing with a spirited gospel number, naturally. "Swing Low Sweet Chariot." A sure-fire toe-tapper even for a backslider like me, thought Jimmie. Born and raised up down south in what they called the Bible Belt,

Jimmie had been hearing good gospel music his whole life, likely beginning in his mama's womb before he was born. The gospel tunes he liked most were the ones they sang about coming into a better life. He did cotton to the notion of another, better life after he left this one he was living here on earth. Staying on the straight and narrow was a challenge. He didn't mind picking out a gospel number or two if someone in the audience made a request. He and the Carters had recorded gospel at a recording session, the last time they'd seen each other.

Jimmie allowed himself a grin at that. Having nipped a few too many that day, he'd crossed over the line, flirting with Maybelle. To no ill effect as it turned out, other than the disapproval of sour old AP. But Maybelle had proven herself to be a good sport about it at this reunion that had brought them all together again.

Jimmie had been born with a wandering eye. Maybelle and Sara were a pair of fine fillies. No doubt about that, thought Jimmie. Thoroughbreds, the both of them. This evening he found himself unable to take his wandering eye from Sara, standing there singing in a stylish black dress that favored her figure. Pretty as an acre of sunflowers. Anyone who wasn't blind could see the distance Sara maintained between herself and her husband.

Jimmie assured himself that his difficulty in keeping his eyes off Sara was nothing improper or off-color. It was something else, not lecherous desire, that intrigued him. While that lovely voice filled the cavernous hall, something in Sara's eyes told Jimmie she was somewhere else even as she sang so exquisitely. Having always been the curious sort, Jimmie couldn't help wondering where Sara's "somewhere else" could be.

The Carters concluded their rousing rendition of "Sweet Chariot."

Jimmie offered up applause along with two stagehands

present to facilitate the sound check. Sara acknowledged the scant applause with a small nod and a smile. Mr. Peer shook hands with the fellow he was conversing with. Concluding their encounter, he walked over to confer with the Carters.

It had been the same after Jimmie had finished a run-through of his set. The idea was for the musicians to get a feel for the famous venue while giving Peer an opportunity to assess the sets his artists intended to perform. Jimmie had thoughtfully structured his song list, highlighting those numbers in his repertoire that sold well on record. He started off with "Pistol Packing Pappy" and kept things up-tempo and on the rowdy side before ending his set with "Waiting for a Train" and "Miss the Mississippi." Peer had approved and then the Carters commenced playing, Mr. Peer listening carefully even after the reporter showed up about halfway into their set.

With the Carter Family and Peer now engaged, the reporter crossed the stage toward Jimmie. As he drew closer, Jimmie did recognize him. A photo of Walter Winchell graced the top of his *On Broadway* column in *The New York Daily Mirror*, the highest-circulation, most widely read tabloid in the city. Winchell's column was syndicated in over two thousand newspapers worldwide. He was read by fifty million people every day. His Sunday night radio broadcast had an audience of twenty million listeners.

Winchell strode up to Jimmie with his right hand extended.

"Walter Winchell," he said. "Got a minute?"

They shook hands, Jimmie worked to make his grip firm. He slapped a big country grin across his face.

He said, "Mr. Winchell, Jimmie Rodgers would be honored to converse with y'all. I've listened to you on the radio many a time, and I always read your column, yes sir-ee."

"Glad to hear it, son." Winchell's speech and manner

were direct, raspy, wholly New York. "I wanted to make your acquaintance. I'll be in the audience tonight."

"Well dang, Mr. Winchell, we'll sure put on a good show for you. Yes sir, you can bet your life on that! Nice to know you got a taste for hillbilly music."

Winchell shrugged his bony shoulders.

"If it's show business, I've got a taste for it." He spoke in the famous fast staccato delivery of his radio broadcasts. "When showbiz gets in your blood, it stays there." His sharp-eyed gaze took in the Western cut of Jimmie's suit and the Stetson. "You look like you just fell off a cattle truck, cowboy. That's a complement. Heard your records. You've got a new look. A new sound Mr. and Mrs. America haven't heard before."

Jimmie said, "Shucks, Mr. Winchell, them songs I write are my own words, sure 'nuff, but my way of picking a tune, well, my style, I guess you could call it, well sir that comes from way back up in the hills and from them old colored boys down south. Reckon I put it all together in a way folks cotton to."

Winchell nodded in agreement.

"This day and age, a performer needs to stand out. What I see in you, son, is a wised-up hillbilly. You're doing fine now, but my friend Ralph Peer intends to take you and the Carters to the next level commercially with this show tonight. From here on out, Mr. Jimmie Rodgers, you're going to be hobnobbing with folks from both sides of the tracks. Get me?"

"I reckon I do," said Jimmie because he didn't know what to say.

Winchell's staccato delivery continued, "Folks out there across America, in the honky-tonk small towns and among the sophisticated set along the Great White Way we call Broadway, you'll be known and respected everywhere you go."

Jimmie said, "Well dang, that's what I've been shootin' for from the very beginning and no mistake. Mr. Winchell, much obliged for your vote of confidence."

Jimmie could listen to talk like that forever. But as he spoke he found himself wondering why is one of the most important men along that Great White Way taking me into his confidence? Hell, if it mattered, really. One mention in a Winchell column or on the radio had lifted many a performers from small time to the heights of stardom...or ending careers crashing overnight from big-time to has-been. Jimmie hardly intended to let *that* happen. This conversation could be his biggest break since meeting Mr. Peer! He was sort of waiting for and expecting the other shoe to drop. Was this a buildup to something good or bad?

Winchell was saying, "Jimmie, you'll be surprised at the range of social circles you'll gain access to. My list of friends and acquaintances range from the stars of Broadway like Georgie Jessel and Jack Benny to gentlemen of, shall we say, more dubious distinction like Dutch Schultz."

"I've heard about him," said Jimmie. "Some kind of bigshot, ain't he?"

"The biggest except for Lucky Luciano. See, cowboy, when it comes to who matters most, I'm like this," he held up an index and middle finger entwined, "with the cops *and* the crooks. The hard part is telling them apart!"

Jimmie nodded.

"Had me the same trouble in them honky-tonk small towns."

Winchell gave a short snort that could have been a chuckle.

"You got to be careful, I'll say that. There's one set of feathers I ruffled with something I said on the radio that could have caused me big trouble. I spotted Lucky in the Cotton Club one evening with a high yellow passing herself for white. I kidded him the next day over the air. Didn't mention any names, just an obscure a little item about a famous local bigshot being a pushover for blondes. Well, Lucky heard it, and he didn't much care for me using the word pushover to describe him. Matter of fact, he was going to send a couple boys over to deliver me a shellacking to set me straight." Another Winchell chuckle. "I had to talk Lucky out of it, and we *are* back to being pals. I've even got his private phone number. But that's how I learned Lucky Luciano does not have a since of humor."

Jimmie said, "Sounds like a dangerous job you've got there, Mr. Winchell."

"It can get that way." Winchell nodded. "See, Tex, Dutch and Jessel and anyone who's anyone along the avenue, what they know off the record and what anyone around them picks up, that's vital to me because the secrets and the scandals along Broadway, that's my meat. That's where the butter for my bread comes from, get me? The more contacts I have, the more information comes my way, the more gossip I have to peddle to my readers and my radio audience. It's what my sponsors demand, and they're the ones footing the bills, and I do mean my paycheck."

Winchell reached into an inside jacket pocket and withdrew a business card. He handed the card to Jimmie.

"There you go, Tex. My telephone number and address, for when you hear something, anything, even if it's just a rumor, that you think I could use. Pass it along to me, big or small. And I'll do what I can for you."

"Sounds all right," said Jimmie. "I'll keep my ear to the ground. I hear anything, you'll hear about it too."

Winchell's hatchet face cracked a small grin.

"You wait and see," he said. "After tonight's show, you'll be getting around more like I said. But now don't think of it as a job, tax, or an assignment. If—let's say *when*—you happen to catch wind of anything interesting, especially if it's anything someone important doesn't want the world to know about, why, get it to me fast as you can. I'll always find a way to return the favor. Fair enough?"

Jimmie beamed his widest smile without trying.

"Sure enough sounds like a no-lose proposition, as we say down home."

"We say the same up here," said Winchell. "Oh and by the way, Tex. There's another newspaper fellow trying to get his start along Broadway. He's patterned himself after me and lately he's been getting too damn aggressive going after a cut of my action. Calls himself Ed Sullivan."

Jimmie said, "Never heard of him."

"Good. If he does come snooping around, tell him to get lost. Don't give him anything you think I can use. Got that?"

"Mr. Winchell, you can count on me."

"Glad to hear it. All right, Tex. Good luck tonight. You're going to have yourself a really big show."

Winchell turned away without offering a handshake or saying another word. He strode across the stage to where Ralph Peer stood conversing with the Carters.

Jimmie had always felt a kinship with the Carter family. Of the nineteen artists who reported at Bristol to audition that day in 1927, he and the Carters alone were deemed to have the "star quality" Mr. Peer said he was searching for. True, Rodgers and the Carters appealed to different audiences commercially, but their careers were running on a parallel track thanks to Mr. Peer working behind the scenes to promote them equally.

By 1927, Jimmie had been knocking around for years playing tent shows, looking for some way to break into legitimate show business. The traveling medicine show circuit was starting to fade but still offered work down south. Jimmie was always pitching himself between his stints working on the railroad. He'd quit singing in a string band to pursue a solo career only a week before he showed up in Bristol.

A week after the Bristol sessions, he traveled to New

York, checked into an expensive hotel and telephoned Mr. Peer to say, "I'm ready for my next session!" That impressed Mr. Peer who immediately arranged another recording session and thereafter served as Jimmy's manager. In just five years Jimmie Rodgers, The Singing Brakeman, had recorded more than a hundred songs, staying busy recording and touring.

With a sweet little wife down home in Texas, a gleaming new Buick sedan ,and a steady income, life would've been perfect...except for the damn tuberculosis that was killing him inch by inch, day by day. He did his best to keep up a good front, but that too was getting harder day after day. He was coughing up blood every morning and every night. Life had become a day to day affair.

How much longer could he last?

CHAPTER EIGHT

TOM DEVLIN ENTERED THE MODERN, marble-floored lobby of an impressive tower of stone masonry and plate glass on Fifth Avenue. The place was immaculate. Upscale. Respectable, as were most of the residents living in the building.

Devlin was thirty-two years old. Dark haired. Five-foot-ten. Heavily muscled. Black slacks, black shoes, and a tan trench coat. A snub-nosed .38 revolver rode in a concealed holster at his right hip. He was a police detective.

He was paying a call on the Dutchman. He was not expected.

Dutch Schultz, millionaire crime boss of the Bronx and Harlem, maintained an elegant luxury apartment on the ninth floor, rented under the assumed name of Russell Jones. He was holed up in fear for his life. Word on the street was that the Dutchman, as he was known, was forcing himself to stay sober so as to be perpetually alert due to the bloody gang war that had been raging across the city for months. A vicious bootlegger turf war with the death toll already over sixty.

Devlin boarded the lobby elevator. The operator sent

him a double take when he requested the penthouse floor. Moments later Devlin was stepping into a carpeted area that sported three doors, one in each of the three walls facing the elevator.

Dutch Schultz's real name was Arthur Flegenhiemer. How he acquired his nom de crime had long ago slipped from collective memory. Born of German-Jewish immigrant parents, the Dutchman quit school at fourteen. His early years were spent running with pickpockets and store thieves. Managing a saloon in the Bronx, by his twenties he had assembled the toughest henchmen in New York, expanding his bootlegging assets through intimidation. His formidable band of hoodlums went about eliminating the opposition, creating a chain of speakeasies, a fleet of trucks and several "beer drop" warehouses for storing the booze.

A pair of musclebound hoods rose from where they sat, one to either side of the door directly opposite the elevator. A bulge under each man's jacket clearly indicated their concealed weapons. Shoulder to shoulder, they glowered at Devlin, blocking his approach to the door behind them.

The one to Devlin's right held up a hand, palm forward.

"Yo, bub. Wrong floor."

They would know the tenants residing in the other penthouse suites.

His partner added, "Scram, chump. It's too late for a social call."

Devlin didn't budge.

"Depends on who's being called on and who's doing the calling. Get in there and tell Dutch he's got company."

"Ain't no Dutch here," said the one on the right. "This is Mr. Jones's residence."

Tom Devlin was a New York native. He'd grown up learning to navigate its diversity, the sheer dynamic *life* of a great city and all it had to offer. Devlin's father had been a New York police office, killed in the line of duty when Tom was ten years old. That single incident birthed a commitment bordering on obsession in the boy to honor his father and the city he loved by growing up to become a police officer. Much as he loved New York, that's how much he hated its criminal element. Thugs like these two who infested his city unchecked, turning its five boroughs into a concrete jungle of human predators terrorizing and victimizing at will its citizenry. Worst of all, New York's legal system was corrupt from the cop on the beat all the way up through city hall.

Devlin gave the hoods a glance at the thin leather packet containing his badge and police credentials.

"I'm here to see your boss. That's me being polite. Take me in to see Dutch, or I'll take myself."

"We'll take you," said the guy on the right. "We'll take you and pitch your sorry ass nine floors down that elevator shaft, that's what we'll do."

"Don't telegraph it," said Devlin. "Give it a try."

They came at him.

The one on the right brought up a fist adorned with brass knuckles while his partner swung a leather sap out and up, arcing it toward Devlin's head. Devlin clamped both of his hands like a vise around the wrist of the arm that was swinging the blackjack. He shoved the wrist back sharply. The sap smacked the man between the eyes with enough force to knock him off his feet, breaking his nose. Devlin then brought the man's arm down across his raised knee. The *crack!* of the arm breaking was loud. The man cried out.

Devlin used the thug's bulk to block the swing coming at him from the brass knuckles. He released the broken arm, letting the first man sink to the floor. Brass Knuckles had momentarily lost his balance. Devlin smashed this one's face into the wall. The thug collapsed, sprawling across the carpet next to his companion, a thin trickle of blood oozing from his broken nose. The sound of ragged breathing filled the air.

Devlin turned when he sensed movement behind him.

Dutch Schultz stood in the doorway.

Thirty years old, the Dutchman wore a black silk smoking jacket decorated with silver dragons. He had the pale, puffy features of a chronic alcoholic. But his eyes were clear and steady with a flinty stare. He held a pistol at his right side, aimed at the floor, his finger around the trigger. Regarding the fallen men, Schultz shifted his gaze up to Devlin.

"Looks like I need to hire me some competent muscle. Who the hell are you?"

"I'm the law," said Devlin. He again produced the leather packet, letting Schultz glimpse the badge. He nodded to the pistol in Schultz's hand. "Lose it, Dutch. Even you won't get away with killing a cop so don't even think about it." Devlin shrugged, and his hands flexed into fists. "Or what the hell. Go ahead if you're feeling lucky. These two boys of yours felt lucky. Make your play."

An icy eye-to-eye stare held between them.

Then Dutch chuckled. The revolver disappeared beneath the folds of his smoking jacket. Footfalls clumped up from behind him from inside the suite. Two more bodyguards. They took in the situation and started for Devlin. Schultz raised a hand, halting them in mid-stride.

"Let him be." Dutch indicated the fallen hoods. "Get these punks out of my sight. Make sure they bounce when you toss them out."

Both bodyguards chimed in unison, "Yes sir, boss,"

They each hoisted one semi-conscious hood over a shoulder and trundled them toward the elevator.

Schultz turned to Devlin.

"You show a lot of brass, pal. You one of the guys the police commissioner picked for his so-called gangster squad? No ordinary cop would dare talk to Dutch Schultz like that."

The police commissioner's creation of a gangster squad had been in response to a fed-up, outraged public and the newspapers' demands for reforming corruption in the police department ranks. The commissioner personally selected a half-dozen of the most trusted officers on the force, men of proven integrity and courage, to form the special squad intended to counter the alarming epidemic of organized crime. Devlin was unit commander of the Gangster Squad.

"Good guess," he said. "The commish wanted to know if I needed backup coming here, another one of the boys to cover me while I paid you this little visit. I told him no." Devlin's eyes took in Schultz with a long up-down sweep to make his point. He added, "I told him I could handle you. I'm one of those tough cops, Dutch. I have the commissioner's blessing to I make my own rules. You're not going to give me trouble, are you? Let's talk."

"Talk or interrogate, I don't give a damn. You've got nothing on me."

"No, but I've got something *for* you. News you can use. Heard about Arn Fratelli?"

"What about him?"

"I heard he'd gone missing."

"So? Arn works for me. So what? I ain't his nursemaid. He does my books. Keeps my taxes paid. My boys run their own lives."

""Well, thought you'd like to know. Arn's not running his life anymore."

"Oh?"

"They found him a few hours ago with the side of his head blown away. Could've been suicide."

Schultz's fists clenched. He had a reputation for having a short fuse. His pale features began regaining color.

"Suicide hell. You coppers know better than that. There's only one guy who's been taking out my guys. Mad

Dog Coll. That sick homicidal bastard likely did Arn in himself! Suicide."

"If it was murder," said Devlin, "it doesn't have to be Coll."

"Oh, yeah? Who else is there?"

"There's you. How have you and Arn Fratelli been getting along lately?"

"What?" A frown from Schultz. "Are you trying to say *I* killed the guy who was keeping my books?"

"Could've happened that way. Let's not forget the Amberg brothers, Joey and Louis. Their brokerage outfit was keeping your books for a while."

"The Ambergs? What about them? Those two stumble-bums skipped town six months ago. I heard their mama took sick somewhere out west so they had to leave town in a hurry. I hope the old girl's all right. That's when I gave the job to Arn."

"They were skimming off receipts," said Devlin. "You had the Ambergs chopped up with an axe and stuffed into trunks and tossed off the Brooklyn Bridge."

Shultz gave another shrug.

"Like I said, you got nothing on me."

"I've got enough to turn up the heat on you if I want to."

"Come on, flatfoot. It's Coll you want, and we both know it. He and his gang kidnapped Fratelli. I paid the ransom. Fratelli's dead. That's what I get for trying to get my man back. Satisfied?"

"For now. According to my information, Lucky Luciano ordered you and Vince Coll to lay off each other. He's the boss of bosses, and he doesn't want you two drawing heat on account that brings guys like me around."

"Is that right? And here I thought you cops were supposed to be busy trying to put that mad dog in the death house after he shot down those children last year. But no, the kill-crazy bastard beats that rap, and now you tell me Arn Fratelli is dead. See what I mean? Things don't always work out the way the way they're supposed to."

"I'm sure Arn Fratelli would agree with you if he could. So have you got anything I can use against Coll that will stand up in court?"

"Tell me another. I live by street law. Vince Coll will be taken care of."

"The way your boys took care of his brother Pete?"

"Yeah, just like that. You said it right. Lucky says there's no money in a street war. But I say different. A damn peace treaty wasn't my idea. Not with a mad dog punk like Coll cutting into our business. I want to see that punk ground up into hamburger."

"You'd go against Lucky Luciano? It's not healthy to cross a Don."

"Lucky's the big boss, no one's disputing that. I'm not crossing nobody except a kill-crazy punk. When Lucky says it's over, I don't like it but okay, I call off my street soldiers. I hole up here with plenty of protection, and you want to know why? It's because I know that mad dog ain't going to honor no peace treaty. Sooner or later Lucky himself is gonna put Coll on the spot. And now poor Arnie. The guy had a wife, you know. A nice girl. Two sweet kids."

"You should've reported it when Coll snatched Fratelli."

Schultz dismissed that with a wave of his hand.

"You want to pin that kill on somebody, hunt down Coll and that conniving, heartless bitch he runs with. She went underground with him. Lottie Kreisberger is the power behind that punk and all his craziness. Lottie could've pulled the trigger her own damn self. Take it from me, that broad is nothing but evil. Damn baby killers."

Devlin reached into a pocket. Schultz flinched, then relaxed when Devlin produced a business card. He handed the card to Schultz.

"We want to take Vince Coll off the streets as much as you do, Dutch. Here's where you can get a message to me fast at either number if—"

Schultz didn't glance at the card. He studied Devlin.

"You sound like a good man, flatfoot. You're pissed off. I like that. Hell man, you're so pissed off about Coll, there's steam coming out your ears." He tore the card into four small pieces. He spat onto the four pieces and flung them to the floor. "But I'll be damned if I need the cops to do my dirty work."

He slammed the door in Devlin's face.

Devlin spoke to the door.

He said, "Fair enough."

His intention had been to throw the Fratelli kill, while it was still fresh, into Schultz's face to see what he could learn, to take his measure. What he'd found made his skin crawl—a conniving, anti-social, amoral thug having risen through the gangdom's ranks through sheer savagery and brutality. Yet given all that, Dutch Schultz was frightened. This of course made him even more dangerous.

Damn right he was pissed off about these sons of bitches. Not only Coll but the whole rotten bunch. The dirty bastards had cost him his marriage. They'd cost him the love of a fine woman and the two beautiful children she took with her when she left, taking the kids to live with her at her parents'.

He had to admit that was better than anything he'd been able to offer them. Life in a big, grimy, violent city was tough from the start for a small town girl from upstate, small town Newburgh. She'd grown up loving the rural life, the open spaces, neighborly folks. She'd come to New York to attend nursing school. She and Devlin met by accident one day and after that, things happened between them the way things do. They fell in love and started a family.

Devlin was the son of a policeman, born to be a cop.

Carol gave it her best. She really did. But the years of anxiety about Devlin on the street and what he was up against, finally took its toll and wore a good woman down. The worst part, she told him, was the goodbye kiss every morning, wondering if she'd never see him alive again. Devlin wanted to make it otherwise. But he was too deeply committed to the path he'd chosen to walk in law enforcement. to serve and protect the everyday citizens of New York who were being exploited and endangered daily by lawless, feuding, dangerous hoodlums who had to be stopped. These opposing issues in his life ultimately cost him his family.

Or had it?

He and Carol spoke regularly by telephone. He was wiring her most of his paycheck every week. He missed her like crazy, and it started eating away at him every time he stopped thinking about work. Carol had resumed her nursing studies at a junior college near Newburgh. The kids were doing fine. Their grandparents loved having the boys around. If he dropped everything and moved up to Newburgh, maybe their little family could be restored. But he couldn't walk away. Honoring the memory of his father made that impossible.

And so hell yeah, he hated these sons of bitches—Coll, Shultz, Luciano, the whole stinking lot of them—with every fiber of his being. These days it was rage and little else that fueled his soul.

CHAPTER NINE

ALONE AGAIN EXCEPT for his two bodyguards in the next room, Dutch Schultz stood before the wide plate glass window that dominated one entire wall of his living room. A bird's eye view of Central Park stretched out like a carpet of green far below. The vehicles and people down there seemed at this distance to be nothing more than bugs.

Dutch enjoyed all of the luxurious trappings that went with being Beer Boss of the Bronx. The penthouse was running him $2500 per month. There weren't many in this so-called Great Depression who could pay rent like that. Men out there were standing in soup lines. Families put out on the street with all of their belongings in the middle of winter because they couldn't pay their rent. Dutch prided himself on having made out all right, clawing his way up from a nothing-to-lose hustling street kid to become Dutch Schultz, boss of men. Feared by many, outranked by few.

There was always a higher rung. For Dutch, that was Lucky Luciano and the "Commission" Lucky was in the process of putting together. Even that could be good thing. The Volstead Act, prohibition, was on its way out according to the newspapers, all but repealed by Congress. When booze was again legal, the whole picture would change. New avenues ripe for extortion and exploitation included labor unions and the entertainment business. Prohibition had allowed the mobs to organize. Lucky Luciano was reorganizing the New York mobs for the future. That made sense. Whatever Lucky and his Commission came up with, Dutch was well fixed politically with much of Tammany Hall already in his pocket. Dutch had done his best to refrain from violence. He'd already coined a phrase heard on the street, "the bribe is mightier than the bullet."

But then there was Vince Coll.

Dutch was putting his faith in signing on with Lucky. Recognizing your own limitations was something Dutch considered essential for any man's success. He'd come of age on the mean streets, rarely depending on anything but his own hot temper and brutal nature. He'd been doing his best to stay on Lucky's good side; to be a team player. But his hot temper, his short fuse, ignited his anger whenever he thought about the punk, Vince. How he'd love to have that maniac's throat in his hands, crushing and squeezing the life out of Mad Dog Coll.

He would never forget the day, three years earlier, when Vince was nothing but a rash kid strutting into one of Dutch's speakeasies only a few nights after the kid's release from Elmira in 1929...

———

VINCE COLL POSSESSED a choir boy image that night. Handsome, tall, and rangy with wavy blond hair, blue eyes, a prow-like nose, and a toothy grin. He was looking for a job.

Dutch knew the type.

Beneath the choir boy façade, he saw the veiled contempt in the young ruffian's eyes even while seeking employment. Dutch knew instinctually how this punk would view him: a smooth, expensively dressed Jew who could be easily conned. The kid said he was willing to do anything, take on any kind of work. Dutch would have to keep an eye on the punk. There was always room in his outfit for a bare-knuckle street tough.

He was about to tell Vince as much when a ruckus erupted on the other side of the speak where Lottie Kreisberger was running her poker game.

Lottie was a piece of work. Claimed to be "a dress designer," though she never seemed to have a real job. For the past month, Dutch had been allowing her to run her game in exchange for a cut of the play. She'd caught his eye from the start. Any man who didn't look twice to savor her stunning gothic beauty just wasn't paying attention.

Her nature was dark, and observing Lottie over time, Dutch had determined her to be a habitual liar, charming when she had to be but in truth an ambitious, calculating, devious manipulator who knew exactly how to use her feminine charms to lead on and control men who caught her fancy, especially the young hothead bruisers who seemed drawn to her like moths to a porch light.

Playing poker in the smoky tobacco haze and dim lighting of a speakeasy, Lottie Kreisberger shone like a polished diamond. Seated at a corner table, her hooded eyes were as intense and focused as those of the four men she sat playing poker with. She had just laid out a winning hand and was starting to rake in a considerable pot of greenbacks.

A man at her table had leaped to his feet, kicking over his chair.

"You damn bitch! You had that ace in one of them boots you're wearing." His glassy eyes dropped to the low cut of her black satin dress. "Or did you hide it between them pretty titties of yours!"

A hush descended upon the speakeasy.

Lottie replied in a quiet, clear voice, "Mister, my titties

thank you for the compliment. But you see, I'm a good enough poker player I don't have to cheat. Now shut your misbehaving mouth, or Mama will shut it for you."

She continued raking in the pot.

The fellow seated next to the accuser placed a hand on the man's wrist.

"Simmer down, Tod. Don't be startin' trouble."

Tod jerked his wrist free.

"I ain't startin' nothing. I'm finishing it. This whore stole my money with her damn cheating ways. She keeps us off balance being so damn pretty and smart."

Lottie said, "Mister, I'm warning you nice. I'll let the whore comment slide because you're drunk. Be on your way, Tod. Say good night."

"I'll say go to hell, whore."

Tod pawed for a concealed pistol holstered at his hip before Dutch or Coll could make a move to interfere.

A derringer appeared in Lottie's right fist, brought up fast from under the table. The right arm straightened. She pulled the trigger. The crack of indoor gunfire was loud. Tod stumbled back against a wall. He remained standing and managed to complete an effort to raise his gun. Lottie shot him again. Tod sighed like a tired man. He slowly slumped down into a sitting position, leaving a wide smear of blood on the wall behind him. He did not move.

The fellow next to him looked on in horror, his shocked eyes glaring at Lottie.

"You killed him! You killed my brother!"

He reached for a concealed weapon of his own, lightning fast before anyone could do anything...except for Vince Coll, who closed in from behind. He grabbed a nearby half-full bottle of whiskey by its neck, swinging the bottle in a wide arc with all his strength. The bottle did not shatter upon impact with the back of the man's head. It crushed skull bone. He collapsed across Tod.

Lottie was stuffing her winnings into her purse.

She said, "Why thank you, stranger."

Vince gave her a sheepish smile.

"Glad to be of service, ma'am."

A bartender came around and knelt over the pair of fallen bodies for a closer look.

He announced, "They're both dead," sounding like a referee announcing the result of a boxing match.

Lottie snickered in Coll's direction.

"He's not talking about us, sugar. Let's get gone."

The brassy young punk hesitated just long enough to send Dutch a quick glance with one eyebrow cocked and a smug smile.

"Well, do I got the job?"

Dutch lifted his eyes from the two dead men. He nodded.

"Yeah, you're hired. Now do what Lottie says." He jerked his head to indicate the speakeasy's rear door. "Make dust, both of you."

The kid fresh from prison took Lottie's hand. Without another word, they exited through the rear door. Patrons of the speakeasy stepped aside, making a way for them as if not having seen or heard a thing. It was that sort of a place.

A few customers chose to leave, but otherwise business at the speak continued uninterrupted.

———

THAT WAS how Lottie Kreisberger met Vincent Coll.

Dutch wished none of it had happened.

He couldn't resist a slight grin at the memory, but the grin became a scowl when he considered the three years since that night. Lottie had been a hustler. Vince, a wild, headstrong punk. The stark truth was that these days not a damn thing had changed.

Lottie was the brains behind the Coll gang. Dutch had no doubt about that. He'd heard it was Lottie who had come up with the original idea of kidnapping other mob guys like Arn Fratelli. It was Lottie's cunning that had transformed Vince from a Dutch Schultz underling into the leader of one of the most feared gangs on the East Coast.

Once Vince had become an enforcer for Schultz, it hadn't taken him long before he started bitching about his low henchman pay. The punk wanted a cut of the action! Naturally Dutch refused.

Vince and his younger brother Pete went behind Dutch's back. They gathered a group of vicious young thugs with the intention of taking on Dutch. One of Vince Coll's friends, Carmine Barelli, was invited but declined to join. Vince shot Carmine and his girlfriend on a public street in broad daylight to silence them. He then set out to decimate Dutch's empire, first by holding up Dutch's beer trucks, beating the drivers with brass knuckles if a driver attempted to fight back. Or Vince would shoot them dead.

Thus began the gang war. Dutch's triggermen had riddled Peter Coll with machine gun slugs a year earlier. Devastated, Vince vowed reprisal. The killings had steadily increased on both sides, the bodies piling up. And now Arn Fratelli, the latest fatality in this war of attrition begun by Vince Coll.

Dutch thought, *So where does that leave me?*

And so he stood at his big picture window, looking down on the world, faced with an untenable situation that would never end until Vince Coll was six feet under. Dutch had never rescinded the open bounty he'd put out on Mad Dog's head. If the punk gets stomped like the snake he is, thought Dutch, would Lucky send his hitmen after me because I disobeyed his edict? Dutch had also clawed his way to become the so-called King of Harlem's numbers racket, the major player in the slot machine business, owner of a string of high-class brothels and a monopoly of the liquor trade. All of that now at risk because of one homicidal little puke, leading to a three-way showdown—Vince Coll, Lucky Luciano, and Dutch.

The telephone rang.

Dutch caught it on the second ring.

"Yeah?"

"You know who this is?"

It was Lucky, his voice smooth as ever with the careful diction of a successful business executive.

"Yeah, Lucky. I know your voice."

"No names," said the boss of bosses. "I just got word one of your men took his own life."

"Fratelli didn't bump himself," said Dutch. "It was that damn Mad Dog. Something has to be done."

"Let's talk," said Luciano.

CHAPTER TEN

VINCE SLAMMED the door behind him on his way out.

Lottie crossed over to the ice box. She used an ice pick to chip away a handful of ice slivers. With every strike of the pick she imagined plunging the long blade repeatedly into Vince Coll's chest. Setting aside the ice pick, she wrapped the shavings in a kitchen towel and pressed the cold towel to where her left eye had been grazed by his backhand the slap.

At least Vince hadn't used his fist. That would have caused a black eye for sure. He'd flown off the handle when Lottie pressed him about where he was going when he said he was going out...*alone*. He told her it was none of her damn business where he was going or when he'd be back. When she pressed the matter, it got her a slap upside the head that nearly knocked her off her feet. Then the door slammed, and he was gone.

Vince had something on his mind.

She knew that much without being told, had first sensed it back at the warehouse when she brought in the Dutchman's ransom payoff. After he'd had his way with Fratelli, Vince hadn't even bothered to stick around to count the loot the way he always did.

Lottie knew her man well enough to know the "something" he was interested in would be something wearing a skirt. Her feelings were even more intense than usual, and the reason was obvious enough. She was about to have her damn period. The cramps had already started. When the womanly curse was upon her, jealousy ruled her dark nature.

She crossed to a window. With her fingertips, she parted the drapery a half-inch from the frame, providing a clear view, three stories below, of the front entrance of the Cornish Arms Hotel where she and Vince had been laying low. She kept a little back from the window glass. If Vince should turn down there to look up, he mustn't know she was spying on him. The bastard would assume she was lying down in the dark to recover from that slap.

The creep!

Only a month ago they'd put in a most natty appearance as an impeccably groomed couple down at the Manhattan Municipal Building, applying for a marriage license. Then they got hitched. *And now he thinks that gives him the right to slap me?* Lottie seethed with rage.

They quarreled often. It was her nature to stir things up. To Lottie's way of thinking, this kept life interesting...and within her control. Unless there was business to take care of, she and Vince were pretty much either screwing or fighting. Sometimes both at the same time! It was a fiery relationship. With two combative personalities, how could it be otherwise?

Vince worshiped the ground she walked on. This was a given, something Lottie knew for fact. And trust in her was absolute, such as in the late night game once played when they were high on whiskey and cocaine, a crazy lovers' role switch reverie she initiated that had her actually place the barrel of her pistol deep into Vince's mouth. Him down on his knees like the gunsel he probably was in Elmira but this time taking her loaded .38, her finger curled around the trigger. Crazy? Oh, hell yeah! A drunken sex power romp proving to Lottie's satisfaction her power over her younger man.

Now she was angry enough to regret *not* pulling that trigger!

Three stories below, Vince emerged from the building onto the busy sidewalk, lifting his collar against the chilly air before stalking off in a determined stride, not bothering to cast a glance over his shoulder up at their window. Lottie soon lost sight of him down there on the crowded sidewalk.

She continued to watch.

Waiting.

No sign of Trigger.

Earlier at the warehouse, after she had overseen Trigger and another of Vince's gunmen relocating Arn Fratelli's remains, she'd taken Trigger aside, out of earshot of anyone else, and had instructed him to discreetly follow Vince. A tail job.

Sure, Trigger was just a kid and not much to look at. But he sure knew how to handle those twin .45s he always wore, a coldblooded killer with a mean streak. He reminded Lottie of her first impression of Vince when they first met. Trigger was learning the ropes, doing what he was told, keeping his mouth shut with his ears and those mean little eyes wide open. Not missing a thing. Yeah, Lottie knew the breed. And yes, she well knew how to bend a boy to her will.

It was a skill she'd been born with and had refined since early in life. Growing up, the boys on her street had all competed for Lottie's attention. She'd see a pushcart candy treat and simply state her desire for it. Whichever boy stole the confection won the prize—her kiss. This graduated to skilled hand jobs for the lucky few but never the ultimate of her "womanly charms." She married into a rich family who paid her to tie the knot with their son to keep him out of military service during the war. She'd divorced the chump by

'25 and had taken up burglary and cardsharping until Vince came into her life.

Trigger had reported back by telephone, informing Lottie of Vince's encounter with a brunette woman in the lobby of the Waldorf-Astoria and about Vince then staking out the elevators, accosting the brunette again. Vince had a friendly conversation with the brunette, according to Trigger.

The fact that Trigger had accommodated her wishes and filed his report told Lottie that she definitely had this boy's interest despite the disparity in their age. His youthful attention and devoted loyalty would follow. That would hardly sit well with Vince, especially if he found out Trigger had betrayed him on behalf of Lottie. Trigger was risking his life if Vince found out.

Trigger supposedly "had some time off." After hearing about the brunette, Lottie had instructed the kid to shadow Vince this evening should Vince leave the hotel without her. Years ago Lottie had once hustled a detective, a Pinkerton man who taught her the basics of following someone undetected. She passed those tips along to Trigger who at this moment was supposed to be stationed nearby, keeping a close eye on the hotel's entrance.

But where was he?

Had this young one double-crossed her? It happened that way sometimes too. Lottie reminded herself that two shoulder holsters of big iron didn't automatically make an iron man. She'd attracted Trigger's interest with demure glances, with expensive perfume to titillate him, and with the occasional "accidental" brush of the back of her fingers across the front of his trousers when the two of them happened to pass within close proximity of each other. This was generally all it took. But she'd been working her grift a long time, and there could be exceptions.

Had young Trigger lost his nerve?

She was seconds away from giving up, from letting the drapery slip from her fingertips back into place, when the kid made his appearance.

Trigger emerged from wherever he'd been conducting his stakeout. He glanced up in the direction of the window where Lottie stood, but of course he could not see her. He started off down the sidewalk, ambling in the direction taken by Vince, apparently with Vince within his sight in the distance, maintaining a suitably discrete distance.

For a beginner at shadowing someone, thought Lottie, the kid seemed to have the knack. Trigger would have made a good detective.

She left the window, removing the ice from her eye. Tossing the damp towel into the sink, she checked herself in the bathroom mirror. The flesh around the smacked eye tingled from the cold press, but the redness was beginning to fade, her natural skin tone returning. She'd avoided a black eye. She poured herself a stiff jolt of Canadian whiskey and nursed it thoughtfully, leaning back against the counter of the small kitchenette.

The bite of the whiskey going down and its heat expanding through her brought her anger to a sharp edge. At times when she was alone, Lottie had long ago fallen into a habit of talking to herself.

She spoke in a tight voice to the empty apartment.

"That slap is going to cost you, Mr. Mad Dog Coll, more than you know. And that goes for whatever little brunette piece of garbage you're out there cheating on me with. She doesn't know it, but that tramp is making the biggest mistake of her life."

CHAPTER ELEVEN

AP WAS fit to be tied.

Sara knew all the signs. She told herself, *Here comes us butting heads again*. She must make quick work of it and deal with this case head-on if she wanted to get away to meet Vince. And that *is* what she wanted. Many things were always running through Sara's head lately, always far more questions than answers. But right now all she wanted was to get away from AP to meet this new, interesting man. And nothing was going to stop her.

After the run-through at Carnegie Hall, Mr. Peer and Jimmie Rodgers decided to "go out on the town." The Carters declined their invitation to join in, returning by taxi cab to the hotel. AP had tersely informed Sara that he wanted a word with her alone, in private.

Maybelle always remained neutral regarding their domestic affairs. With a free hand she relieved Sara of the autoharp case. Sara nodded her appreciation. With the autoharp case gripped in one and her guitar case in the other, Maybelle proceeded without comment across the hallway to the room she was sharing with Sara. Behind her, Sara and AP stepped into AP's room.

At age 40, Sara's husband could easily have been mistaken for a man twenty years older. Tall, somber, and gangly, he nonetheless carried himself with a sense of importance. He'd suffered since childhood from a physical tremor as well as a constitutional restlessness which his mother ascribed to a near miss by a bolt of lightning when she was pregnant with him. AP rarely spoke or smiled unless he had to and never with a wasted word. The music he supplied and arranged for their group meant everything to him, and AP in turn expected everyone else to share his enthusiasm for the performing and recording career Mr. Peer had opened for them. AP's emotions ran deep, Sara more than anyone knew that, yet he never seemed able to express them until moments like this.

When they were alone, he said, "Sara, it just ain't right."

"What ain't right, AP?"

She'd manufactured the impression, during the returning ride from Carnegie Hall, that she was exhausted, ready to turn in for a nap to refresh before tonight's performance. In reality, she'd been unable to think of anything except her upcoming get-together with Vincent.

AP said, "You know what I'm talking about. It ain't right, you being my wife, and here we are in New York City in a big fine hotel. And you're rooming with your sister-in-law! You oughta be right here in this here room, sleeping with me like the married folks that we are. When we're out there in public, you act like we're married, I reckon. So why the blazes are you spending your nights across the hall, not wanting to sleep with me like I got me some sort of horrible disease? It ain't right."

"Well get used to it. It's over, AP."

"Over?"

Sara was surprised at the sudden, brief pang of sympathy she felt for this poor man. She'd been a good wife even when she did not love him. Now he didn't even have that.

"You and me, AP," said Sara. "I'm done with it. Whatever we had, it's long gone and done with. You'd better start getting used to it. I'm sticking for now because of the act. I can't let Maybelle down. But as for you and me, we're finished, and you dang sure shouldn't need no telling why."

"It's that dang Coy."

"Stop. You leave Coy out of this. Everybody knows that's over and done with between him and me."

"Yeah. Everybody. Everybody knows everything about us, don't they? I was a-hoping after your Coy and his folks lit out, things would get back to the way they once was 'twixt you and me."

"Well, that's just never going to happen, AP. Don't you know what *over* means? Them old times between you and me are over. And you know what? They never should been in the first place."

"Aw now, don't be saying that, Sara."

"I'm only saying what's true. I never should've married you, AP. I was nothing but a restless, innocent young girl wanting to get away from home."

"Wife, you misremember things." AP's expression and tone lightened. "I can't stop thinking on them days when you and me was sweet on each other."

"I never was sweet on you in my heart, AP. Not ever. Not really. We're nothing alike, you and me. You shuffle around all the time like man half dead or in a trance. I've still got plenty of life in me, and I ain't wasting no more of it on you."

AP spoke as if she had not.

He said, "I was working selling trees and shrubs for that nursery, remember? Traveling the county, staying with the locals, playing music on the porch after dinner. Then one day—it was eighteen years ago, Sara, but I remember it like yesterday—me walking down a mountain path I'd never been down before when I heard the most beautiful singing voice I'd ever heard."

"Stop," said Sara. "It's too late for that kind of talk, AP. I don't want to hear none of it."

AP said, "And there you was on the front porch of your family place. Sara, I'll remember that picture in time for long as I live. You singing a railroad song about the death of a train engineer. Remember? At my request you sang it a second time. I was captivated. The most beautiful voice I'd ever heard and the most beautiful woman I'd ever seen."

"Hardly a woman. I'd just turned 16."

"Then came those 10-mile hikes over Clinch Mountain to court you. I could have ridden a horse, but I love walking, and you was worth it, Sara. You was worth it. A day to walk across, I'd take my lunch, spend the night with friends and walk home the next day after spending time a-courting you."

"AP, you're wallowing in your misery like a hog in mud."

"Sara, I've never stopped loving you the way I did then."

For another heartbeat, Sara felt a twinge of guilty regret for the hurt she knew her words must cause him. But then she thought of Vince waiting for her downstairs in the tea room. She blinked away such thoughts.

"Live in the past if you want to," she said. "I don't care. You never should have left me and the kids alone to freeze and starve last winter when you took off hunting for your dang songs."

"Those dang songs took us out of the poor house," said AP, "and they're keeping us and our kids fed these days, ain't they?"

"I ain't going to spend another minute standing here arguing with you, AP. That's all in the past. I'm living in the here and now. And I'm rooming with Maybelle. Good night to you."

She didn't give him a chance to respond. Letting herself out of his room, she resisted the urge to slam the door behind her. She must get away from him, not escalate the situation.

Across the hallway in the room she shared with Maybelle, Sara's autoharp case rested atop her bed. The sound of a running shower and the humming of one of their tunes from behind the closed bathroom door indicated Maybelle taking advantage of one of the Waldorf's prime luxuries.

Sara leaned over the writing table, drawing the sheaf of Waldorf stationary to her. She wrote, *Don't worry about me. See you soon. S.*, across the sheet and placed it atop Maybelle's pillow. It was a relief not to interact with Maybelle before going out. Maybelle, bless her heart, would certainly not approve. Checking and quickly touching up her appearance in the wall mirror, she let herself out.

Walking along the corridor toward the elevators, she restrained an impulse to hurry. She mustn't draw attention to herself. What if AP should somehow appear and start asking questions? That didn't happen, thanks heavens, but even walking at a normal pace her throat became dry, her heart pounding against her ribcage. She was only a short elevator ride away from seeing him again! What would happen next between the attractive city man and the head-strong mountain woman?

But what if he wasn't there?

What if Vince was not in the tea room, waiting for her? She would feel like such a fool. She told herself, *No! He is downstairs, waiting for me.*

CHAPTER TWELVE

AND THERE HE WAS.

Poised. Confident. Seated at a corner table halfway back in the Waldorf's tea room, a comfortable, dimly lighted, tastefully appointed oasis in the hurry-hurry world of New York, warmly inviting with its elegant atmosphere of exclusivity and class. Most of the tables were occupied by couples and small groups amiably chatting and imbibing. Waiters in tuxedoes glided about efficiently, refreshing beverages and serving up light snacks.

A maître d' started forward when Sara entered but drew back upon seeing that she was already approaching Vince's table. The very sight of Vincent sitting there waiting for her, and she forgot all about AP and everything else. A chill of anticipation was coursing through her. She even forgot about Coy!

When she reached his table Vince rose to his feet, smiling that sweet choirboy smile of his that charmed her so.

"I was hoping you'd show up."

"I hope you haven't been waiting long."

"If I had, it would've been worth it. You look lovely."

"Thank you, Vincent."

"And I have an idea."

"Oh?"

"I'm a hardworking gent. Worked hard for every penny I've got." He glanced at their surroundings with an expression of distaste. "I feel sort of out of place around all these high-roller types, if you know what I mean."

Sara felt a small stab of disappointment. She knew what he meant about feeling like an outsider amid all this elegance. But truth was she'd been looking forward to elegance as part of this illicit adventure, being waited on in this lap of luxury. But Vince was a successful, hardworking man who obviously had his pride. She did not want to spoil anything.

She said, "I'd love to go wherever you wish, Vincent. Did you have a place in mind?"

"Matter of fact," said Vince, "it's just around the corner not far from here. We could relax there and be more ourselves. What do you say?"

His enthusiasm was contagious.

Sara told herself to relax. It was likely a better idea to go somewhere else anyway, Sara told herself, to avoid anyone she knew around the hotel seeing her in the presence of a gentleman who was not her husband. Vince expected her to say yes. She must not disappoint him.

She said, "Lead the way," adding with a small self-conscious grin, "I'm a stranger in these parts."

They left the tea room, skirting the lobby toward a side exit short of the main entrance and front desk. Sara felt pleasantly swept along.

But then it happened.

They were almost to the double doors of the side exit when those doors opened inward, and who should come strolling in from outside but Mr. Ralph Peer and Jimmie Rodgers! Sara's heart skipped several beats, seeming to leap into her throat with panic.

The two men were in high-spirited conversation,

enjoying each other's company. Jimmie, animated, seemed to be telling Mr. Peer one of his tall tales. Mr. Peer was listening with obvious amusement. That is, until he happened to catch sight of Sara from the corner of his eye just as she and Vince were on their way out. In those few seconds before they lost sight of each other, Sara clearly saw his amusement turn into puzzled surprise.

It happened so fast, with Vincent not noting them as anyone Sara knew, so she decided to say nothing to him about it. But it was unsettling. She didn't know what to think. Then they were out on the busy Manhattan sidewalk. Vince picked up their pace. She kept pace with him.

He said, "We're not far. Cold, isn't it?"

"Not like down home," Sara heard herself say.

His arm went around her, drawing her close as they walked.

And now she *really* didn't know what to think! The sudden, unexpected physical nearness of him drove home what it was she was doing. She was a married woman no matter the state of that marriage. What was she doing, adding this to her life, meeting to chat with an interesting gentleman? And here he was with his arm around her as if they were already on intimate terms...*in public*!

The brownstone storefront he guided them to was set back from the other buildings along this block, making for a sort of courtyard that gave way onto the sidewalk. When they reached an unmarked doorway at the far end of the courtyard, Vince knocked on the door. A slot in the door clicked open at eye level, and a pair of eyes looked out. The eyes must have recognized Vince. The door swung inward. A shabbily dressed fellow stood there, a cigarette dangling from the corner of his mouth.

"Evenin', Mr. C." He made a broad gesture of invitation. The cigarette bobbed as he spoke. "Always good to see you. Come right in."

Sara experienced another stab of uncertainty. This fellow knew Vince. He assumed they were a couple!

Vince told the man, "We're looking to warm up, Fritz. Got us a table?"

"This way, Mr. C!"

The doorman led them through a smoky haze of rough-hewn tables and rough-looking customers openly drinking from bottles of beer and shot glasses. A colored man was playing piano discreetly from somewhere in the club. The lighting in here was dim, that being the only similarity to the Waldorf tea room just around the corner. Snatches of conversation heard in passing were coarse and profane.

Sara's nagging sense of unease continued to build. She told herself to ignore the pestering of her subconscious. Moonshine was naturally everywhere back home in the hills. What with revenues being scarce in them parts, sure, a body could find a speakeasy easy enough in the larger settlements. But the Carter Family did not patronize nor perform in such places. It was plain enough to see the bad effects on a person and on a community that could be brought on by the consumption of alcohol. Ruined lives. Battered women. Fatherless children. Men fighting and killing. Sara had hoped to enjoy this bit of not-so-innocent adventure, getting to know an interesting gentleman. She had not expected to be brought into a lowlife speakeasy.

With only the slightest smile to herself she thought, *Maybelle would throw a fit if she saw me here!*

Sara sought to reason with herself. *Don't be harsh on Vincent because he patronizes a place like this. So they know him in a speakeasy. So what? You've come this far, Sara. This is no time to turn chicken-livered! Stay with it!*

By this time Vince was holding a chair for her to take, a most gentlemanly gesture before seating himself across from her in a secluded corner somewhat removed from the rough-hewn atmosphere of the place. Vince sensed her discomfort.

"We'll be okay here," he assured her. "What would you like to drink?

"You'll laugh at me," said Sara, "but I think I'll just have a glass of soda water."

"You call that living it up?" Vince chuckled. He said to the doorman, "A glass of white wine for the lady. I'll have the usual."

The doorman/waiter said, "Got it," and disappeared into the smoky dimness.

"I wish you hadn't done that," said Sara, not unkindly. "I'm a grown woman, Vincent. I can make my own choices."

"Sorry," said Vince. "My mistake. Won't happen again. I'd like our friendship to be perfect."

"What a nice thing to say," said Sara. "Oh, I'm sure it will be." The minor irritation melted. She chuckled self-consciously, thinking of Thanksgiving and Christmas holiday celebrations back home, "And this won't be my first glass of wine," she added with a smile.

The waiter reappeared with their order. Vince's "usual" was a shot of rye and a beer chaser. He handed the man some folded bills. The fellow's eyes widened when he saw the amount.

"Thank *you*, Mr. C!"

He withdrew to return to his post at the front entrance. Vince clinked his shot glass to Sara's wine glass.

"Here's to us."

"To us," Sara repeated.

Sara took a sip of her wine. Vince threw back his shot. After a sip of beer, he reached across the table to place his left hand upon hers, radiating expansive contentment.

"Now we're living! What do you say, sugar?"

His familiarity of manner was increasing with each word. Sara thought about removing her hand from under his. But she did not wish to offend, and truthfully, the gesture of possessiveness was not altogether unpleasant. Strangely, his touch...his touch had a chill to it. She should learn more about this man before this went much further.

She said, "You're a favored customer here. You must come here often."

Vince brushed that aside with a shrug.

"Often enough. You're not going to write a book about me, are you?"

"No, of course not. But you know how curious women are. It would be nice to know something about you."

He took another sip of his beer.

"Not much to tell," he said. "Twenty-three years of age. Born in County Kildare, Ireland. Orphaned. Me and my brother Peter were brought over to the States by our sister. She did her best raise us."

Sara felt herself relax some, comfortable now discussing family.

She said, "So you're not alone. That's good in big old world like ours. I imagine life in a big city like this could get lonely without family. Where are Peter and your sister now?"

That brought a chill to Vince's eyes, impossible to read.

He said, "Let's talk about you."

She should have expected that. But she hadn't. She'd been so caught up in learning about Vince, she hadn't quite realized that he would be just as interested in her.

"I . . . I don't quite know what to say about me." She wanted to kick herself for stammering like a schoolgirl. She thought for a second, and then pushed on with the first thoughts that came to her. "We're mountain folk," she said." That is me and my husband, AP, and my cousin Maybelle. I heard tell the Appalachians are the world's oldest mountains and Clinch Mountain—that's where we hail from—why, they say Clinch Mountain is the oldest peak. I don't know, but that's what they say. People farm mostly. Along the bottom lies Poor Valley where the soil ain't so good. That's where AP and his people are from. Rich Valley, on the other side of the river, is where I come from."

Vince cocked an eyebrow and grinned.

"Poor Valley? Rich Valley? Sounds like that old man of yours married up in class, you ask me."

"AP's got his ways," she conceded, "but when it comes to music, well, that man he knows what he's doing, I'll say that for him."

Vince seemed to be listening keenly with no change of expression.

He said, "You don't see many musical trios from Tennessee playing at Carnegie Hall."

"That's AP's doing, getting us to where we are." Sara nodded with some pride at the mention of the upcoming performance. "It's been a long journey from Maces Springs, our little home town, to this concert, sure enough. I only wish I could enjoy the whole rigmarole more than I do."

"How long have you been at this racket?"

Sara thought, *racket?*

She said, "We've been working regular about five years." She emitted a sigh that sounded weary to her own ears. "Sometimes it feels like lifetime. Other times it feels like yesterday when we got started."

"Tell me about it."

"I don't want to be just making talk. Are you really interested?"

"Yes, I'm really interested."

"Well, it took some doing, but AP talked me and Maybelle into making the drive to Bristol where the fella who became our manager was holding auditions. Pshaw, me and Maybelle, we'd always been happy just singing on the front porch for friends and family. But AP come up with the notion we could make a living with it. Took us an entire day to drive the twenty-six miles from Maces Springs to Bristol, traveling them dirt roads that ran up and down among the foothills. The road hadn't been graded in a while and was nothing but twenty-six miles of washboard."

Vince chuckled.

"Sounds like you were lucky to even have an automobile."

"Maybelle's husband was paid well working as mail clerk on the railroad. He was the first person in the Valley to own a car! AP had to practically get down on his hands and knees and plead to borrow that car for the drive to Bristol. AP had to agree to hoe the weeds out of their corn patch. And what a drive it was!"

"Life in the backwoods, eh?"

Sara nodded.

"I'll say! Maybelle was eight months pregnant. Me and AP had our three children. I took along my baby Joe who was still nursing and Gladys, our oldest, to help out with things. Poor Maybelle. We had to stop to answer her calls of nature every mile or so. A tire blew. AP, he got a rubber patch over the inner tube, but the heat kept melting it away so we had to stop twice more for him to re-patch and pump air back into the inner tube. But we made it, and the upshot in Bristol was us getting a contract to record our songs for The Victor Talking Machine Company. And here we are."

"And here we are," Vince agreed. "This husband of yours sounds like an enterprising fellow. Me and you seeing each other like this, should I be worried about AP?"

"Let me worry about my husband," she said, hoping to assure him as well as herself.

She'd talked about AP quite enough. She couldn't help but chuckle at the notion of someone being "worried" about AP in the way Vince meant. The short speech about her own life she'd just served up had somehow emboldened her. Why should she be the one to do all the talking?

Vince must have read something in her expression.

"What is it, Sara?"

She gave in to her curiosity. Taking a deep breath, she plunged on.

"Vincent, what do you do for a living?"

CHAPTER THIRTEEN

VINCE TOOK another sip of his beer. He flashed his fresh young man smile.

He said, "So she wants to know how I to make a buck," adding, with an offhand rise and fall of his shoulders, "Oh, a little of this and a little of that."

Sara had left her wine untouched.

"No, I mean really."

"Stop," he said, wagging an index finger in her face. "There are things we don't need to talk about."

"Maybelle says you're a gangster."

Sara gasped, surprised at the words that had just left her mouth. Vince's manner softened. The chill in his eyes gave way to an amused glint.

He said, "Maybelle is right. But it's a bum rap, as they say. That's the name they had hanging on some of my associates, I'm embarrassed to say, but as for me I'm simply in the business of supplying a public demand. Folks should be able to have a drink of wine or beer or hooch if they're not causing trouble for other folks. It's not easy for a poor boy from the slums to make it in this world."

Sara wasn't sure what to think. She was amused. He was so straightforward rather than protesting!

She said, "Back home making and selling moonshine can be a mighty dangerous business."

"It's no different in the city," said Vince, "and you can bank on that. I know there's a bullet out there waiting for me. What other way should I expect to check out?"

"So I'm in danger sitting here with you?"

"It's a dangerous world, kitten."

"We live in different worlds, don't we, Vince."

A thoughtful look came into Vince's eyes.

"Don't think I wouldn't like my world to be different. I like sitting here talking politely with a woman of class."

"Oh, please."

"No, I mean it. You're real good person, Sara. In my line of work, I can't be the way I really am. Show an inch of kindness, and they'll mow you down. So I force myself to act like a tough guy."

"We do live in different worlds," she insisted gently, "but we have the same problem, don't we? I'd like to get to know you, Vince. You've been ever so polite, listening to me and all."

"It makes for good conversation. You haven't touched your wine. Do I make you nervous?"

"I don't know. I was just thinking perhaps I should be getting back."

At that moment Vince saw something over her shoulder, and everything changed. In an instant his friendly, relaxed expression dissolved to become a harsh stone mask she barely recognized.

He muttered an audible, coarse expletive at whatever he saw that shocked Sara who'd spent her life around profane, plainspoken working men. She thought she knew most of their curse words. But the curse that escaped from the corner of Vince's mouth was vulgar beyond anything she'd ever heard.

A man in a trench coat appeared from behind her to stand at their table. A man of average height, powerfully built, he cast a hard glance down at Vince.

Vince spoke first with a sneer.

As if Sara was not present...

He said in a raised voice, "Damn, it smells bad in here all of a sudden. I thought this was supposed to be a respectable joint. No cops allowed." He waved his hand in a dismissive gesture. "Don't bother showing me your badge. I can smell a copper a mile away even if he is in plainclothes."

"Name's Devlin," said the man in the trench coat. "I'm just from having a talk with Dutch Schultz."

"Oh, yeah? How's the Dutchman doing?"

"Looking over his shoulder from what I could see. Laying low in that penthouse of his. Seems to think someone's out to get him."

"Imagine that. So what's that got to do with me?"

Sara sat listening to the words passing between these men sparring with each other. Conversation from the surrounding tables had died down to nothing. Even the piano player had stopped playing.

This was no place for her to be!

She had to get away. It wasn't far to the hotel...

"Vince—," she started to say.

But his full attention was on the man standing before them.

He was saying, "Take a hike, copper. You're just fishing, harassing me in public." He finally acknowledged Sara's presence with a thumb thrown in her direction. "Can't you see I'm on the town with a lady?"

Vincent's sneer now looked like a permanent fixture on his face.

The man, Devlin, said, "I suppose you've heard Arn

Fratelli, one of Dutch's boys, got put on the spot. Dutch says it was you're doing."

"Yeah, well, Dutch is just trying to make trouble for me, and you damn well know it."

Devlin appraised Sara with a direct gaze that managed to be respectful, in no way judgmental.

"Lady, you're keeping bad company here."

She returned his gaze.

"I beg your pardon?"

"I say that," said Devlin, "because you look to be a respectable woman. You don't mind my saying so, you ought to be more careful about who you spend your time with."

This unexpected turn of events, the aggression passing between these two, caught her by surprise, stunning her. Her heart felt caught in her throat, her world upended topsy-turvy in the time it takes to flip a coin. She eyed the entrance across the smoky, dim speakeasy where the doorman stood tending to his duties.

Across the table from her, anger had flared in Vince's eyes.

"Stow your noise, flatfoot, or there's going to be trouble."

Devlin's response was a snort.

"From you? I don't think so." He spoke to Sara. "Take it from me, ma'am. Bums like this are all mouth and no guts, only good enough to shoot down a man in the back in a dark alley." Returning to Vince, he added, "I've heard about you, Coll. You don't look like much to me. Nothing but a small-time crook posing as a big-time racketeer. You ought to leave respectable people alone."

Vince finished his beer. He set the mug down with a thud.

"You're measuring yourself for a coffin, Detective. Anything more you want to say or do before I shut you down?"

Sara's mind was racing: *Sara, what the blazes are you doing here? Run!*

Devlin's lips curled at the corners in what could have been a smile.

"What am I going to do? I'm going to do what I'd do to any cheap gun who thinks my hands are tied up with red tape. Make a move I don't like, and I'm going to slap you down like the misbehaving punk you are."

Vince bolted from his seat in a burst of rage, his hand darting under his coat. But not fast enough. Devlin's right hand was a blur as it swept up to smack Vince across the left cheek. Not a very hard blow, but everyone in the crowded speakeasy heard it. Vince's tall frame trembled visibly, his head jerking sharply. His whole body seemed to tilt. Then Devlin's left hand came up, and its open palm rocked Vince again.

They stood facing each other, Vince visibly angry but holding himself in check with a grimace.

He said in a low, tight voice, "Devlin, damn your soul and mark my words. You're a walking dead man. I'm going to kill you for what you just did."

"Not today," said Devlin. "I'll track down whoever killed Arn Fratelli, and they'll answer to the law. I hope it's you."

While the pair of them stared each other down with every eye in the place transfixed by the confrontation, Sara rose to her feet. No one seemed to notice. She intended to edge her way into the crowd as unobtrusively as possible. She must leave this place! She must return to the Waldorf and the safety of the world she knew.

An abrupt eruption of activity from the front entrance interrupted everything, reflexively drawing everyone's attention including Sara's. She tried to make out what was happening.

A pair of men had forcefully gained entry past Fritz, knocking down the doorman on their way in. They flung aside their overcoats, revealing that each man held a heavy weapon. One held a shotgun, his accomplice, a Thompson submachine gun!

They opened fire. The speakeasy exploded into a thundering, flaring inferno.

The angry chatter of the machine gun and the awesome booming of the shotgun hammered Sara's eardrums. The first thing she saw was Vince Coll pitching himself to the floor to escape the gunfire sweeping the club. Bullets buzzed over his head.

The police detective, Devlin, assumed a low crouch, filling his hand with the a .38 automatic from his shoulder holster, dodging well away from the table. He was looking about, searching for Sara in these first seconds of chaos as the crowd reacted into blind mass of human panic. Everyone was pushing for the exit.

The gunmen concentrated their fire on the table where Devlin had confronted Vince and Sara. The hail of bullets struck a half-dozen or more onlookers, the volley sending people toppling this way and that. Bullets blew apart flesh, filling the air with splattering blood. The gunfire continued unabated, drowning out screams of pain and death.

Sara threw herself into the scattering crowd.

The closest gunman to Vince momentarily paused to yank back the lever on his chopper, preparing for another extended burst of automatic fire. Vince took the brief opportunity to rapidly trigger three rounds that sounded insignificant after the hammering of the machine gun and shotgun. The three rounds struck the gunman—two in the torso, one between the eyes. The shooter dropped his machine gun as he was flung back, spraying the wall behind him with his blood.

Meanwhile Devlin shot the second gunman, catching this one in the process of racking the shotgun. Two rounds lifted off the top of his head, dousing those near him with his brains and skull fragments.

The chaos swirled everywhere, people shouting, scrambling, cries for help from the wounded and dying. The agonized howling of the badly wounded. Pure bedlam.

Devlin rose to his feet, maintaining his low crouch in the tightly packed confusion pushing around him. The exit was funneling the crowd out too slowly, resulting in a mad press of everyone clawing to escape the carnage at once.

He saw no sign of Vince Coll or the woman.

It was the woman who concerned him. He'd had the impression of someone in well over her head in the company of Mad Dog Coll. He had intended to confront Coll merely to size the guy up but had proceeded to slap him down in front of others so as to leave no doubt that this cop was not bought or intimidated by anyone toting a gun. But for now, he could find Coll again any time he wanted. His interest in the attractive brunette was personal. He wanted to find her if he could, to make sure she was free of any consequence of her involvement with a mad customer like Coll.

Devlin started to elbow his way through the dense human madness, angling toward the front until the mass of humanity seemed to become blocked by some sort of obstruction ahead. This did not deter the panicky mob from jostling him from every side. Then he tripped over something or someone, he couldn't tell who or what in the dense dimness, driving him to the floor.

Within seconds he was swallowed by darkness, feeling like he was being trampled by a stampeding herd of buffalo.

CHAPTER FOURTEEN

SARA TRIED to conceal herself among the people pouring from the speakeasy into the courtyard that fronted the building. Her heart was racing. The sight of men and women being blown apart under a hail of gunfire overwhelmed her. Country folk on the farm were no stranger to death—animals, crops, people—but the horrible reality of human slaughter drove her blindly with everyone else. Anguished howls of the wounded and dying rang in her ears.

The human flow had already made it outside. They scattered.

She dodged behind a billboard advertising an adjacent business, concealing herself alone there rather than risk revealing herself by continuing with the others across the short distance to reach the sidewalk. They made it out, and Sara realized maybe dodging wasn't such a great idea. The courtyard now appeared empty.

Vince appeared in the doorway of the speakeasy, blocking the customers trying to push their way out. He stood there as if firmly planted, a pistol in his hand, his jaw set in a look Sara had seen back home when men fell out and set themselves to killing. Vince looked ready to kill. His eyes panned left and right across the seemingly vacant courtyard. Searching...

Sara remained hidden behind the billboard, not moving a muscle, holding her breath as if the very act of breathing might tip Vince off to her presence.

Then he saw something.

Vince left the doorway, stalking forward with a determined stride. But not in Sara's direction. He stalked with his determined stride toward another business billboard on the opposite side of the courtyard. As he approached, a figure darted from behind that billboard, making a mad dash for the open sidewalk.

Fritz, the doorman!

Fritz only made it two or three steps with a frightened scream before Vince's long left arm reached out, his fingers gripping the doorman's collar, throwing Fritz to the ground. Fritz gave up trying to escape. He scrambled around on his hands and knees to look up at Vince. He clasped his hands together as if beseeching heaven itself.

"Mr. C, *wait!* I didn't do nothing! Please don't hurt me!"

Vince glared at Fritz down the length of his arm, his pistol aimed directly between Fritz his eyes.

"Didn't do nothing?" Vince spat a grimy wad of phlegm that struck Fritz's forehead, remaining there unattended. "Those shooters knew exactly where I was sitting. You tipped them off, you lousy little fink."

"Mr. C, I swear I didn't know what they were up to. They said you were expecting them. I didn't know I was doing something wrong. Please, *please* don't hurt me!"

"Hurt you?" Vince gave a short laugh. "I'll see you in hell, punk."

Fritz cried out, *"No!!!"*

. . .

VINCE JAMMED his pistol's muzzle into the gaping *O* of Fritz's mouth, breaking teeth. He squeezed the trigger three times. When Fritz toppled sideways onto the pavement, the back of his head had been blown into a bloodied mass that began pooling on the pavement.

A few curious citizens had begun cautiously gathering. They now went diving for cover.

Vince stood there for only an additional second or two, the pistol in his hand. He was in a hurry to get away, but he took a final second to scan the courtyard one more time. His eyes sped over the billboard behind which Sara was hiding.

Please, please, Lord, don't let him see me!

Vince did not see her. His main concern now was to depart. He hurried away. Anyone who saw him coming dodged aside to escape his path. He stalked off down the sidewalk, away from the speakeasy and the Waldorf-Astoria. Then he was lost to Sara's sight.

She promptly vacated her place of concealment, avoiding a glance in the direction of poor Fritz. Onlookers were advancing with less caution now that the killer gone. While their attention was on the dead man, she hurried away.

CHAPTER FIFTEEN

LOTTIE KREISBERGER SAT by the window, waiting for the telephone to ring. Her body and mind fed on an anger roiling through her like liquid fire.

Damn. She wanted to *kill* someone or something! Break something valuable into little pieces. She could feel herself vibrating with a hostile intensity that kept building without release. She'd smoked the last of the reefer in the apartment and snorted up the last of the cocaine. It was risky business scoring the stuff up in Harlem, and Vince would be angry when he got home to learn he'd have to make another trip to score. Then she thought, the hell with Vince.

Where was he anyway?

Why hadn't Trigger called?

She resented this sitting around, waiting. The coke made her premenstrual cramps worse. They were tearing up her guts. The reefer sometimes helped her, but this time only heightened the nasty mood that had her in its grip.

At least she had her private flask. She unscrewed the cap and took a taste, liking the way the whiskey burned going down, stoking the fires of restless rage. How nice it would be to just walk over to the cupboard in their small kitchenette.

She'd take out plates and hurl them against the wall with all her might just to see and hear them shatter. But of course she could not do that.

She and Vince were lying low here at the Cornish Arms, pretending to be a respectable husband and wife. She couldn't raise a ruckus that would draw attention. The cops were always looking for Vince.

Fond as she sometimes allowed herself to feel about the guy, recently she had started wondering if their relationship was becoming too much of a liability for her. Maybe it was time to find a new man, especially if Vince was out chasing skirt.

There was Wilbur, a.k.a. Trigger. She gave a snort of derision at herself. Would she stoop that low? The kid was likely a virgin. A bad case of acne. Only nineteen years old. No, anyone she picked to take over from Vince would need a hell of a lot more seasoning than Trigger. Still, the boy had already agreed to follow Vince and his brunette. Lottie could use him, nineteen or not. She must be damn careful. Vince was dangerous as hell.

The phone rang.

Lottie answered with a simple, brusque, "What?"

"It's me."

Trigger sounded out of breath.

"Where the hell are you? What's going on?"

"Hell's a-poppin.' I followed the boss to the Waldorf where he met up again with that brunette."

"The son of a bitch. And Trigger, you know he's not the boss, right? You're talking to the boss right now. Got that? I think you're smart enough to already know what's what."

"Uh yes, ma'am. Uh, I know."

Lottie thought, good enough.

"Well, what happened?"

"Uh, everything sort of blew up and went haywire."

"God dammit, quit pussyfooting around, boy. Where'd they go?"

"They went to a speakeasy around the corner from the Waldorf. I couldn't chance the boss—I mean Vince—I couldn't chance him spotting me so I hung around outside, figuring they'd have to come out sooner or later."

"Speed it up, Trigger. What the hell happened?"

"Well, everything went crazy. All kinds of shooting from inside the speak! People come flying out of there. It was so crazy I couldn't make out who was who, and I had to be careful about staying back. That's when something really crazy happened. Mr. Coll, he comes out and finds some guy hiding. He shoots the guy. Shoots him to death right there in broad daylight! Then he goes hustling away and guess what?"

"What, Trigger?"

"The brunette he was with, she puts in an appearance but not with him. She was hiding too, and once Vince is gone, she takes off in the opposite direction. I followed her."

"And?"

"She came back here to the Waldorf. That's where I'm calling from. I can see her from this phone booth. She's queued up by the bank of elevators. It's a crowded mess. A long line. So I ducked into this phone booth to call you."

Lottie had been keeping an eye out the window, watching the street and sidewalk below. When she caught a glimpse of Vince approaching the front entrance of the residential hotel, she knew she had to act fast. "Trigger? "

"Yes, ma'am?"

"For a man who does what I tell him to do and gets the job done right, I can be very nice. Do you understand what I'm saying, Trigger?"

"Uh, er, yes, ma'am. I guess I do."

"Good. Be that man for me, Trigger. I'll be nice to you.

When we're alone, I'll do things you can't imagine. Things you'll like."

Across the connection she clearly heard Trigger's heavy breathing.

"Uh yes, ma'am...uh, what do you want done?"

"Hang up the damn phone. Move your ass, and make a way to ride up in that elevator with her, whoever she is. Can you do that?"

"If I hurry. Then what?"

Vince would be more than halfway up the stairs to their apartment.

Lottie said, before she hung up the phone, "Don't come back until that bitch is dead."

———

DEVLIN STOOD next to the police commissioner at the edge of the sidewalk, watching medics load the last of the bodies into an ambulance. The vehicle sped off, away from in front of the speakeasy.

Winter was returning with dusk, the spring-like temperatures of a sunny day yielding to the chill of approaching night.

Commissioner Tuchman was burly, gray-haired, and nearing retirement age. Despite holding a prestigious bureaucratic city hall position, he retained a strong feel for everyday street-level police work dating back to his own days as a patrolman. Tuchman had about him a seasoned, no-nonsense air of command. He lit a cigar, his eyes on the receding, flashing lights of the ambulance, its siren wailing.

"Wonder what the big hurry is. Those folks aren't getting any deader."

"Maybe the drivers just want to make tracks away from this mess," Devlin said with a nod to cluttered scene around them.

There in front of the speakeasy, police officers were doing their best to hold back the crowd of curious onlookers that always gathers to gawk at the scene of a violent crime. Newspaper reporters were in attendance, shouting a steady barrage of questions at the officers. The courtyard in front of the speak was inundated with cops questioning survivors of the shootout while others snapped photographs of what physical evidence they could find.

Six bodies had been carted away: the pair of gunmen who initially opened fire, three innocent bystanders who'd been seated at adjoining tables, and Fritz, a panhandler hired to work the door. Another dozen gunshot victims were rushed to the hospital, several with life-threatening wounds.

"The dead gunmen are good riddance," said Tuchman. "The hoods are doing our work when they rub each other out. But when decent folk can't go out to relax without something like this happening...it's got to stop, Devlin. And it's our job to stop it. First that little boy who was killed last summer during a mob hit. Now this. If Jesus walked around New York today, he'd never stop puking."

Devlin said, "Vince Coll is the key. If he's not perpetrating violence, he's drawing it to him, and innocent people pay with their lives."

"Any idea who sent the gunmen responsible for this?"

"We may never know. Maybe they sent themselves. A pair of freelance gunnies trying to cash in on the fifty-grand bounty Dutch Schultz put out on Coll's head. Things won't cool off until Coll is dead and gone. That's what Dutch and Lucky Luciano and the other big boys think, and they're right."

"He's a slippery son of bitch," said Tuchman. "Tom, I want that punk Priority One."

"Someone's going to take him down and soon," said Devlin. "Everyone knows it, even that kill-crazy Coll, if he's even capable of a lucid thought at this point. I came down here to take his measure. After what happened here, I'm cutting to the head of the line to be the one who shuts down his crazy show before anyone else dies."

"This woman who was with Coll. Could she be a lead?"

"Maybe. That is, if we knew what's become of her. Sir, that brunette wasn't one of the cheap, common dames you see hanging out with hoods. She was a mature, attractive woman. A good-looking woman."

"She seems to have made quite an impression on you."

"She has. I can't quite explain it, but the impression I got the minute I walked up to their table was that she didn't quite belong, and she knew it. She shouldn't have been with Coll in the first place. She found that out in a hurry. Then she disappeared."

"To where, I wonder," said Tuchman. "Are you smitten enough to find out?"

"You mean track her down? Sir, without a name, there's nothing to go on. She didn't say a word. But she is a key witness. Yeah, it would be good to see her again."

Something about this "mystery woman" who'd been with Coll in the speakeasy did stir Devlin in a way he couldn't quite put his finger on. She hadn't spoken a word but had managed to radiate a decency far above the setting of a drab, common speakeasy.

Smitten? Not hardly. They were separated, but that didn't mean Devlin wasn't still in love with Carol, the woman who'd borne him two sons. With everything else going on in his life, thoughts of her crossed his mind every day since she took the boys and moved back to her folks. He might idly think of the way she would brush her hair back from her forehead. Or the way the boys had acted like a pair of happy monkeys after the family went to see *King Kong*. His little family, apart though they were, was always with him it seemed.

No, not smitten. Devlin chuckled to himself. But who was the mystery woman? Would they ever meet again?

CHAPTER SIXTEEN

JIMMIE RODGERS SAT in the lobby of the Waldorf-Astoria, paging idly through the *Daily News,* one of the city's juicier tabloids. He felt restless. But he was on a mission, staked out in this majestic hotel lobby at the request of Mr. Peer who'd suggested the newspaper to make Jimmie "less conspicuous." Jimmie's mission—keep an eye out for Sara Carter.

His eyes had barely glanced at the newspaper. For one thing, he didn't give a hoot in hell for most of the hoo-hah they ran in the news these days. The goings-on of them scoundrels down in Washington made our nation's capital a snake pit any way you sliced it. It's why he kept his repertoire down to the basics—romance, dreams, regret, and good times and leave politics out of it.

Earlier, when he and Mr. Peer had been returning to the hotel, coming in through the row of doors at a side entrance, they'd spotted Sara and a tall young fellow passing on their way out. Jimmie had been concluding an off-color joke that had Peer chuckling. Moments later when they were about to catch an elevator, Peer's expression grew serious.

"Did you see Sara just now?"

"Sure did. Didn't recognize that feller she was with."

"I want you to do me a favor, Jimmie."

"Why sure, Mr. Peer. Just name it."

"Okay, here it is. I recognized that man from his picture in the newspapers."

"Is that right? They seem to be enjoying each other's company."

"Here's what I want you to do. Park yourself in one of those plush armchairs over there. Sara will be returning, I'm sure of that. When she does, you hang back. We don't want her to know we're mixing into her private business."

"But we are mixing in, is that it?"

"Afraid so. For her own good, of course. You see, that man she was with is a notorious gangster."

Jimmie gave a low whistle between his teeth.

"Dang. You think she's in danger?"

"I don't know what to think," said Peer, and you could tell it was not an admission he was used to making. "When Mrs. Carter does return, I would like you to see that she gets up to her room safely without her knowing. Think you can do that, Jimmie?"

Jimmie wanted to ask few questions. Like, who was the feller they'd seen Sara with? Seemed kind of odd for her to be steppin' out alone, when she should have been accompanied by Maybelle or AP in the interest of propriety.

And say something untoward did happen between Sara's arrival here and making it to the room she shared with Sara? What the heck, Jimmie wondered, was he supposed to do about it? Sure, he was packing a rod. Is that why Mr. Peer entrusted him this task? What sort of trouble he was taking a hand in?

He preferred to be doing things and going places. Sitting in a stuffed chair, waiting for something to happen, wasn't Jimmie Rodgers's way. He almost fell asleep twice, jerking his head erect and giving it a shake to revive himself.

He considered the flask of moonshine that rode in his coat pocket, acquired from a grubby hanger-on at the train station when he arrived in New York. Thanks to Mr. Peer's generosity in picking up the tab everywhere they went and letting Jimmie order as he wished, there had been no need to avail himself of the flask. He admonished himself for even considering taking a jolt on the sly.

Then he caught sight of Sara Carter, hurrying through the side entrance located to Jimmie's left. Even from that distance across the lobby, Jimmie got the impression she was flustered, striding toward the bank of elevators.

He set aside the tabloid, wondering what to do next. As always, or so it seemed, a large number of people formed a queue to board the elevators. There seemed to be a waiting time of several minutes, the line of people moving steadily but slowly. He started in that direction.

Then he noticed the young fellow, couldn't have been more than nineteen or twenty years old, his face scarred with acne. There was something vaguely menacing about the way both his hands remained deep in the pockets of his long coat. As the line grew shorter he advanced, only three people behind Sara, staring straight at the back of her head.

Jimmie hurried toward the elevators, nearing Sara from her blind side as she became the next in line. One of the elevators opened. Its passengers poured out. When the car was vacated, Sara and those behind her began moving forward to board the elevator. Since she and the seedy young fellow wearing the long coat were among the first in, they positioned themselves along the rear wall of the car, the young man to one side while Sara stood at the other as the car filled up.

Jimmie picked up his pace, rudely cutting in on the final person about to board so that he, Jimmie, was the last one on board. He avoided making eye contact with Sara, facing forward. The elevator boy eased the doors shut, and the car began to rise.

Jimmie recalled that Sara and Maybelle were staying on Floor Six. So when someone aboard called out "Five please," he exited the elevator along with those getting off on that floor. When the elevator doors closed behind him, and his fellow passengers dispersed in either direction, Jimmie rushed to the stairwell between floors. He pushed the door open and his long legs scrambled fast as he could up the concrete steps three at a time. The only sound was the echo of his footfalls and the rasping of his ragged breathing.

Reaching the door to Floor Six, a wave of dizziness swept over him. He had to grip the metal door handle to steady himself. His shortness of breath, gasping for air, was incredibly loud in his ears. But that's just me, he told himself. It took only a few seconds for him to restore his normal breathing. No more than a minute had elapsed since he'd left the elevator one floor down. He inched the stairwell door open just far enough to squint through.

The corridor stretched in either direction. There was the elevator in the opposite wall, the grinding sound from the shaft and the row of indicator lights meant it was well on its way to the next floor up. Further down along the corridor, he saw a couple in the process of entering their room. There was no one else in sight. Another corridor led straightaway from the elevator. This was the one that ran past Sara's room.

Jimmie bolted from the stairwell, rounding the corner seconds later.

Sara stood at the door to her room and was in the process of trying to insert her key into the lock, wholly unaware of what was happening behind her.

The young man in the long coat was stealthily advancing, raising the long blade of a switchblade knife, seconds away from plunging it into Sara's back.

CHAPTER SEVENTEEN

NO TIME TO STRATEGIZE.

Pure instinct took over.

In healthier times during his railroading days, Jimmie had played some football. Nothing professional, just off-time, rough-house scrimmaging. When he saw the scene unfolding before him, he gave a loud shout to get the fellow's attention, throwing himself at the kid in a tackle worthy of those bygone railroad days.

He piled right into the guy full force, bumping into Sara Carter in the process, almost knocking her off her feet. She uttered a small cry of surprise and alarm. Jimmie's arms going around the guy's legs. The sheer momentum of the tackle sent both men skidding across the plush carpeting. The kid's first response was to kick Jimmie hard in the chest, booting the air out of what was left of Jimmie's TB-ravaged lungs, breaking the hold Jimmie had on the kid's legs. They gained their footing together, Jimmie with slightly more speed because he wasn't wearing a long, bulky coat. As the young man straightened, he shifted his grip on the knife, no longer ready to plunge its blade but rather to lash out as in a street fight.

Jimmie had learned long ago that the best defense was an aggressive offense. He flung himself at the guy in a full frontal assault, blocking a swipe with the knife. His left ankle twisted around the guy's right ankle. Another full-force shove and again they both went down. Jimmie's one hand gripped the wrist of his opponent's hand holding the knife. He delivered a short, sharp punch to the young man's jaw, not hard enough to knock out the assailant, but the punch did daze him, giving Jimmie an opportunity to use both hands to twist the wrist of the hand holding the knife. The kid cried out. The knife dropped from his fingers.

Jimmie leaped back up to his feet. He coughed a couple times but, thank God, it was not one of those times when he coughed up blood.

He snapped, "Stop right there, son. What the hell's going on here?"

The nearest rooms' doors, facing each other, opened. AP stood in his doorway, frowning. Across the hallway, Maybelle stood holding Sara in a protective embrace. The eyes of both women were wide with shock and confusion.

The assailant snarled a graphic curse at Jimmie, who stood over him. The coarse words came out slurred from that sock to the jaw. But instinct had the kid pawing under his long coat. He could only be reaching for a gun.

Jimmie had hoped like hell it would not come to this. Now he had no choice. The kid was drawing his weapon, encumbered by the long coat. Jimmie yanked out his silver automatic with the fancy pearl grip. He stepped in close enough and pressed the muzzle against the young man's forehead.

"When I say stop it, I mean stop it, dag-nabit."

This got the guy's attention. He froze.

"Don't shoot," said the kid. "You got me cold. We can work this out."

"What's your name, son?"

"My name's Wilbur."

Jimmie held the upper hand but did not intend to press his luck. Wilbur, crouched before him with the gun to his head, was still capable of turning the tables. Jimmie hardly considered himself a tough guy. He recorded songs like "Pistol Packing Pappy," but that was only an act to sell records and concert tickets. True, he'd done his share of hard, honest labor on the railroad and had consorted with a fair share of rough customers. But he'd never before been in a situation like this.

He stepped back a few steps, the pistol holding its bead on the spot between Wilbur's eyes.

"We'll work things out after you hand over your guns," he told Acne Face. "Use your fingertips. Draw those guns out slow. Place 'em on the floor between us."

Wilbur did as he was told, setting a pair of large automatics on the carpet midway between himself and Jimmie. The pistols looked absurdly out of place surrounded by the grandeur of the hotel's corridor.

"Satisfied?"

Jimmie's finger remained curled around the trigger.

"AP, get his guns. Hand one to me."

AP left his doorway and stepped forward without speaking, maintaining his unreadable façade. While he didn't share Jimmie's familiarity with firearms, as a man of the hills, AP was not uncomfortable in their presence. He scooped up the automatics, one in each hand. For a heartbeat, given his formidable stature and stoic countenance, AP Carter reminded Jimmie of some two-fisted, two-gun hero off a cowboy pulp magazine cover. AP handed one of the guns to Jimmie, who pocketed his own pistol and aimed the heavy .45 at Wilbur. AP went to stand with Sara and Maybelle.

Maybelle said, "Will someone please tell me what the blazes is going on here?"

She was ignored. Wilbur appealed to Jimmie.

"Look, mister, let's you and me talk business somewhere private, just you and me. What do you say?"

Jimmie considered this. It was a miracle no one had come along in the short time of this encounter, which had unfolded swiftly and without much noise, not drawing the attention of anyone beyond the Carters. And this was about as far as Jimmie wanted to pursue the matter. This was a job for the hotel's house detective at least, more likely for the New York PD. Either way, his involvement was as a favor to Mr. Peer. That made Peer the man in charge. He might prefer this business to be swept under the rug to avoid scandal and bad publicity for tonight's show. The most expedient thing to do at present was to detain Wilbur and notify Mr. Peer of this situation.

Jimmie said, "Okay, AP, here's what we're gonna do. You go fetch the boss."

AP's stoic eyes glanced at Wilbur.

"What about him?"

Wilbur's eyes were on Jimmie.

"You ain't gonna kill me, are you, mister?"

Jimmie lowered the pistol, though his trigger finger remained in place.

"And bring the whole joint down on us?" He bent his knees and retrieved the knife Wilbur had dropped. He slipped the knife into his pocket and gestured with the gun toward the open doorway of AP's room. He said, "In there. You came here looking for trouble, cousin, and you dang well found it."

Wilbur stepped past Jimmie, into the room. Jimmie cast a glance to where the others stood grouped in the opposite doorway. Sara appeared to be in a trance, her eyes glassy, her jaw slack. AP's countenance remained stoic as if sculpted in granite. Lively intelligence animated Maybelle's appraisal of the situation.

She said, "I'm still waiting to hear what this is all about."

"I've got a hunch," said Jimmie, "Sara could tell you a heap more about it than I ever could."

He followed Wilbur into the room, closing the door behind him.

As if on cue, a man and a woman emerged from their room three doors down. They walked by with polite nods, passing the Carter Family on their way to the elevator. AP was still holding Wilbur's pistol at his side. He shifted it to behind his back so they wouldn't see the weapon as they walked by. When they were beyond earshot, Maybelle spoke.

"Sara, honey, what's going on."

Sara said nothing. Her glazed eyes registered nothing.

AP said, "This is intolerable. We need to get things straightened out and fast."

"Never knew you to do anything fast, AP," said Maybelle with a trace of vinegar in her voice. "Go fetch Mr. Peer like Jimmie said."

"Jimmie will do all right for himself. You saw that rounder handling a gun on that boy Wilbur. I will fetch Mr. Peer sure enough," said AP. "But before I do," he said as his eyes stared daggers at Sara, "we're going to have us a private family meeting."

CHAPTER EIGHTEEN

SOON AS THEY were alone in AP's hotel room, Wilbur warmed up as if they were pals making conversation, yakking back and forth as if Jimmie was not holding the .45 at his side, presently aimed at the floor but with the safety off.

Wilbur said, "Thanks, buddy, for getting us offstage. But just out of curiosity, are you the house dick?"

Jimmie couldn't resist a chuckle.

"Naw, I'm the feller usually getting the bum's rush from the house dick."

"Then we can talk business."

"Is that right?"

"Sure is. Let's you and me talk quick before this Mr. Peer shows up."

"You can forget about that," said Jimmie. "Trying to bribe me, is that it?"

"Hell yeah, that's it." Wilbur reached for his back pocket. Jimmie tensed, thinking the kid was reaching for another concealed weapon. He relaxed when Wilbur said, "I've got five hundred bucks here with your name on it just for letting me walk out of here." He showed his wallet, spread open to reveal the sheaf of greenbacks. "Forget this happened, and you've earned yourself five hundred smackers."

"Forget what happened? Fella, you came at Mrs. Carter with a knife, trying to kill her sure looked like. A feller don't hardly forget something like that."

Wilbur said, "They call me Trigger. I'm warning you, high hat. I got friends who'll make your life a living hell if you don't let me walk here and now. You talk like a hillbilly. Does that make you stupid? Get smart, rube. Let me go."

"I believe we can dispense with the name-calling," said Jimmie.

He studied the hotel room. It matched his own. Artful wallpaper and expensive furnishings including a bed, an armchair, and a writing desk with a wooden chair against one wall. Jimmie's eyes settled on a closed closet door. A walk-in closet similar to the one in his room. Jimmie nodded at the door.

"Closet," he said.

Trigger frowned.

"What about it?"

"You're getting inside it. That's where I'm holding you until they decide what to do with you."

"Hell, I ain't getting in no goddamn closet."

Jimmie hefted the pistol.

"I might be a rube, but this rube's got himself a gun. When you got a gun, people are supposed to do what you tell 'em to. Damn it, Trigger, get in the gol-dang closet."

Trigger paused to scrutinize Jimmie, sizing him up. Easy to see he was trying to make up his mind. Would Jimmie blow a hole in him if he felt like it? Trigger was figuring the angles. He read something in Jimmie's eyes and decided resistance was not a chance worth taking.

"Hillbilly, you know damn well it won't take a lawyer but three seconds to spring me from any cell they toss me in, right? Welcome to my town, country boy. Now be a smart rube. Earn yourself some easy money, why don't you? Give me back my guns and let me go."

The closet," said Jimmie.

"Now hold on. What if I suffocate in there?"

"You won't."

"Yeah, but what if I do?"

"You tried to kill my friend Sara with a knife, damn you. Do as I say, dang it. You're getting me riled."

The kid stepped into the closet. But he was not happy about it.

"It ain't human, doing this. That's it. It's inhumane is what it is, dammit!"

Now that the guy was doing as he was told, Jimmie felt the slightest twinge of sympathy before shutting the door. He knew what it felt like to be locked up. That sort of thing stays with a man. During his railroading days he had on occasion rode the rails as a hobo. The railroads don't much care for hobos. Jimmie had been thrown off trains. He'd been arrested for vagrancy and thrown into the jug more than once.

He reached into a pocket with his left hand and withdrew the flask of whiskey. He extended it to the kid.

"Tell you what. Keep your yap shut, be a good fella, and you can keep company with this."

Trigger, a.k.a. Wilbur did not lose his dark glowering attitude. He did, however, snag the flask from Jimmie's hand.

"That'll do, I guess."

He unscrewed the cap and took a long pull.

Jimmie closed the closet door. He reached over and drew to him the wooden chair from the writing desk. He positioned the chair on its back legs so that the back of the chair angled under the doorknob.

He said, "Try to get out."

From inside the closet, the kid turned the knob and tried to force open the door. The chair securely held the door in place, preventing it from opening. Trigger muttered a foul, imaginative curse.

"Good," said Jimmie. "Now behave."

He settled into one of the armchairs, placing the .45 on the chair arm. He felt satisfied with himself. But did not relax. Mr. Peer would be along shortly to take charge. Nothing to do now but wait.

He found himself wishing he had not handed over the flask.

CHAPTER NINETEEN

WHEN HER WORLD WENT TOPSY-TURVY, Maybelle had been sitting on her bed in her nightclothes, idly strumming her guitar, not playing anything in particular, just noodling about to keep from thinking about Sara.

They had long ago forged a deep bond between them, not hampered by the fact that Sara was years her senior. They'd been through much together first as childhood cousins, then as grown married women even before music took them from the hills. Sara was good people. A strong woman...that is until last summer's fling with Coy Bays.

It was starting to look like maybe the thing with Coy was more than a fling. Oh, it was over sure enough what with Coy and his family now settled on the other side of the continent. But Sara hadn't been the quite same since the affair ended.

Drying off from her shower and finding Sara gone had left Maybelle ill at ease. A scribbled note left behind. What could Sara be up to out there in big bad New York? It would have something to do with that fellow Vince, that was a sure bet.

When Maybelle heard a faint metallic scratching at the

door, she set the guitar aside. That would be Sara. Strumming the guitar had done nothing to ease her thoughts of concern. The faint rattling indicated difficulty inserting a key. Maybelle rose and crossed to open the door.

Sara stood there looking disheveled, the room key in her trembling hand. Her eyes were vacant in some sort of daze. She started to say something.

Without warning, two hurtling male figures collided so close to Sara that she was jolted violently, almost knocked off her feet, bumping directly into Maybelle's arms.

One of the scuffling men was Jimmie Rodgers!

For a few seconds it was like something out of a Western movie. Jimmie and a young man in a long coat, tussling across the carpeted corridor, Jimmie performing with a show of strength, agility, and speed Maybelle would never have imagined him capable of.

So now, minutes later, Jimmie and the young ruffian were behind the closed door of AP's room across the hallway. Maybelle sat on the arm of the chair in which Sara sat leaning forward, hugging herself, trembling as if with a terrible chill. Maybelle's left arm rested across Sara's shivering shoulder while her right hand held Sara's hand. Sara's eyes were still glazed. She had said nothing.

AP, towering over them, demanded of Maybelle, "What do you know of this?"

"No more than you. She went out not that long ago. That's all I know."

"And you let her go out alone?"

"I didn't know she'd gone out. I was taking a shower."

"You know how she's been lately. You should be keeping an eye on her."

"And why's that, AP? Your wife is a grown woman."

Maybelle instantly regretted not biting her tongue. But AP ignored the remark. He stood with his hands on his hips, glaring down at Sara who sat shivering, staring at nothing.

The two of them reminded Maybelle of a hardnosed cop interrogating some frightened witness.

AP said, "Sara, you are not to continue with this behavior." The heat of accusation burned in his every word. "Woman, I am your husband, and you will do as I say. What sort of deviltry is this?"

Sara did not respond.

Maybelle said, "She was attacked, AP. That young man came at her with a knife. Jimmie came to our rescue. We're not going to learn anything with you being so harsh."

"And what would compassion get me?" grumbled AP. "More of the same?" His scrutiny of Sara registered something he hadn't noticed before. "Is that blood on the hem of her dress?"

Maybelle stroked Sara's tousled hair as if she were comforting a child.

"All will be revealed. Right now Sara needs to relax."

"No," said AP. "No more keeping me in the dark. Maybelle, I know you side with Sara on just about everything. But I demand—"

"You can demand all you want, AP. You always do. But didn't I hear Jimmie tell you to go fetch Mr. Peer?"

"I don't take orders from that rounder."

"Now you're being downright foolish. Stop being ornery and stubborn as a mule. If we don't want word of this to get out, we can't trust talking on the telephone. Do like Jimmie told you and go fetch Mr. Peer."

Their eyes clashed and held for the time it took AP to consider this. Once he had, he turned and left the room without saying another word.

The change in the atmosphere of the room was stark once Maybelle and Sara were left to themselves. For a short time the only sounds were those of the New York traffic, vaguely audible in the distance. Here in their hotel room, that whispering background noise became soothing. Sara's tremors receded to a deep, ragged breathing. At last Maybelle's patience was rewarded.

At last Sara lifted blank, empty eyes. "Oh, May..." A tearful plea.

"Oh, May..."

Maybelle placed a maternal kiss atop Sara's head and said, "Tell me all about it, hon. What happened?"

———

IT DIDN'T TAKE LONG for AP to return with Mr. Peer, for which Jimmie was grateful. During the interim, Trigger had not made a peep from inside his closet, apparently satisfied with chugging away from the flask Jimmie had given him. Jimmie hadn't lost sight of the fact that at any second his prisoner could grow rambunctious. The .45 automatic was reassuring, but Jimmie did not want to shoot anybody.

Peer promptly took charge. He dismissed AP, who left with a visible show of relief to rejoin Maybelle and Sara. Closing the door after him, Peer eyed the closet door, and the chair propped to keep it shut.

"Now then, Jimmie. What have we got here? AP wasn't too sure."

Jimmie delivered his report briefly and concisely, from spotting the kid in the lobby, up through the knife, the scuffle in the hallway, concluding with an offhand comment about handing over his flask to the punk. Jimmie felt himself starting to relax now that he was no longer in charge. The Rodgers way was easygoing good times and good music, unlike Mr. Peer who seemed invigorated by Jimmie's report. After hearing Jimmie out, Peer nodded his approval. He indicated the gun resting on the arm of Jimmie's chair.

"Very good, Jimmie. You did well. Do we have a name?"

"Wilbur. Wants people to call him Trigger."

Peer spoke to the closet door.

"Wilbur, are you all right in there?"

The reply came at once.

"Hell yes, high pockets. I'm more than all right." Inebriated belligerence dripped from every word. "Ain't nothing going to stop me, you got that? I been sitting in here on my rusty dusty waiting for you to show up, sport. You heard the hillbilly. The name's Trigger. Got that? That's what they call me. That's who I am. Trigger."

Peer rolled his eyes at Jimmie.

He said, "All right, Trigger. Tell me why you came at Mrs. Carter with a knife."

That brought a drunken chuckle.

"You sound like a lawyer, sport. You a cop?"

"Call me an interested party. I want to know what happened and why. Why'd you do what you did?"

"You gonna turn me over to the cops?"

"Maybe. Maybe not."

"You sound like a bigshot. Okay, bigshot, put this it in your pipe and smoke it. I'm one of Vince Coll's boys. You do know who Vince Coll is."

Peer's hesitation surprised Jimmie, who'd never heard the name before. But it sure did register judging by Peer's uncertain expression, his initial reaction before the business-like demeanor returned.

"Yes, I know who Vince Coll is."

"Then let me the hell out of this damn closet, sport, or you're in big trouble. You got that? By the way, who are you?"

"You don't need to know who any of us are, Trigger. You already know enough for your own good. Just tell me why you did what you did. Then I'll decide what to do about it."

From inside the closet came a muted clunk, the sound of a flask dropping to the floor.

"Tell you what, high hat." Trigger's slurred speech was becoming more noticeable with every sentence. "Why don't you and the hillbilly just let me out of this goddamn closet? We can make friends. I'll spill whatever you want to know. Sure will. What do you say to an offer like that, big man? Just let me out of here, why don't ya?"

Peer said, "Thing is, Trigger, we'd be satisfied if you went away and never came back. We could then continue living our lives, and my friends will leave town tomorrow. But I must know what happened and why before I can decide how to handle this situation you've presented me with. Was your attack on Mrs. Carter personal, or did your boss order it done?"

Wilbur said, "Aw, jeez. Why can't you just let me out? It's dark in here."

Wilbur sounded like a pouting little boy. He kicked the closet door but without much force. There followed a rustling thump, a collapsing sound that could only be Wilbur drunkenly tripping onto the closet floor.

Peer said to Jimmie, "Here's how I see it. If he's some star-crazed fan who has it in for our Sara for some crazy reason, and if he's drunk on his ass, well, I'd say let's get him out of the hotel and leave him someplace where he'll sleep off his drunk in an alley somewhere and forget about this. But if his attack on Mrs. Carter is somehow tied to something else, something bigger that could pose a direct threat to us, well, in that case we'll have to risk the publicity and take whatever steps are necessary."

"You mean like go to the police?"

"Yes, even that. Mrs. Carter's safety is the only real concern. Nothing is more important than that."

"And after the show?" said Jimmie, "Me and the Carters, we'll be getting the hell out of this town. But for right now, Mr. Peer, uh, where does that leave me? I was sort of hoping—"

"I'll work fast, Jimmie. You remain here. Stand guard over our friend Trigger just a while longer, won't you?"

From within the closet could be heard the humming of a barely recognizable Rudy Vallee number.

"He's not going anywhere," said Jimmie. "Sounds right harmless at the moment, don't he? Don't reckon he'll get a second wind. That flask I gave him did its job."

"He will be out of commission for the time sufficient unto our needs," said Peer with a nod. "And you're armed, Jimmie. Don't put yourself into any personal danger, understand? I'm going across the hall to have a talk with the Carters."

Jimmie scratched the back of his neck.

"Reckon I'll be glad when this is over and done with. Don't you worry none, Mr. Peer. He'll be here when you get back. Jimmie Rodgers is on the job."

CHAPTER TWENTY

PEER STEPPED into the room and surveyed the situation with a seasoned eye. AP closed the door and remained standing with his back to it. Maybelle had never left Sara's side. Maybelle was grateful for Peer's arrival since it ended the awkward silence that had reigned in the room since AP's return, the three of them waiting for whatever was to come. Sara was no longer trembling, yet there remained about her the appearance of one not quite present. Faraway eyes stared at a distant horizon no one else could see. When Mr. Peer asked, Maybelle went ahead and told him what she'd learned from Sara during the brief time the two women had been alone before AP rejoined them.

Sara had told Maybelle her story in a flat monotone, reciting a string of incredible, stunning events. Meeting the fellow, Vince. Him taking Sara to a speakeasy. The massacre. As she listened to Sara's fitful recitation, Maybelle recalled having heard sirens from the street outside, and she now knew the reason.

Peer stood in the center of the room, feet firmly planted, arms folded across his chest, listening to every word with a stern countenance. AP remained at the door, dour of demeanor, taking it all in. Sara sat staring straight ahead without speaking, disengaged as if Maybelle was talking about someone else.

Maybelle concluded with, "And that's all Sara has told me. Reckon for now she don't want to talk about it no more."

AP cleared his throat. "Reckon it's time to call in the police, you ask me."

Maybelle wasn't sure what to think of that idea. She said, "What should we do, Mr. Peer?"

"When I saw Sara leaving the hotel with Vincent Coll of all people," said Peer, "I should have taken steps immediately. The fact that I didn't was my big mistake. I did ask Jimmie to watch over Sara once she returned. I'm so sorry, Mrs. Carter. I should have acted promptly."

Maybelle said, "Jimmie saved Sara's life, and you were responsible for having him there. We're so glad for that. But what about the man with the knife?"

"We're facing a tricky situation here, I'll grant you that," said Peer with a frown. "Especially since the fellow we have in custody claims to be in the employ of Vincent Coll. If we were in some little town or a nice small city, yes, I would take this straight to the authorities. But we're in New York. Frankly, the power of the criminal element in our city is such that if a Vince Coll wants to cause trouble, he will."

"Do the police know about him?" asked AP.

"They do," said Peer. He sighed. "As do the newspapers and everyday newspaper readers such as myself. Last summer Vince Coll allegedly participated in a gangland assassination attempt that resulted in the shooting death of a child. Children were playing outside an apartment house. A limousine pulled up to the curb, and someone with a machine gun opened fire on an enemy gangster. The human target threw himself to the sidewalk, and four young children were wounded. One of them, a five-year-old boy, later died. The cops arrested Coll, and he was tried as being the gunman who opened fire. The prosecution fell apart in court and Coll beat the rap. That's when our mayor, Jimmy Walker, dubbed him a mad dog."

"Well then," said Maybelle, "what are we going to do?"

"Mrs. Carter will be safe with us," said Peer. "She'll be among us from now until after the concert and after that, until you folks leave town in the morning. That being the case, let's avoid bad publicity. The Carnegie Hall concert is intended to expand the base of your audience, to bring your music into the lives and homes of hardworking, everyday citizens. Much time and money has been invested in tonight's undertaking. Any association like this with criminals and their ways would have a detrimental effect. Very detrimental."

"This is Sara's life we're talking about," said Maybelle. "In this whole big city, I can't believe *every* officer of the law is corrupt. Isn't there one policeman we could trust?"

"You're right, of course," Peer nodded. "The corruption of which I speak is fought by the newspapers and reform politicians. I'm told the current police commissioner is determined to weed out corruption. Perhaps I could—"

Sara spoke.

"There *is* a policeman in New York I would trust." Her words came in little more than a whisper. "I haven't mentioned him. Everything is coming back so fast. So awful, everything I saw..."

Maybelle said, "Of course, dear. Take your time."

Peer said, "But tell us. What's his name? "

Sara said, "His name is Devlin."

CHAPTER TWENTY-ONE

WHEN DEVLIN GOT word the police commissioner wanted to see him, he was winding up a hastily called meeting of the Gangster Squad.

Devlin knew better than to think in terms of painting police corruption with too broad a brush. There were many good cops risking their lives every day and night on the mean streets of the city. Trouble was, their number was equaled by the bad apples—bought-off cops who infested every level of the department from the neighborhood beat cop right on up through the ranks to include precinct captains and even those in administrative positions. It was becoming increasingly difficult knowing who to trust. The handful of men comprising Devlin's elite squad were men above reproach, a handpicked crew of plainclothes officers representing the very best of New York's Finest.

The meeting had been called to compare notes, to form a general picture from the street rumors circulating in the wake of the speakeasy massacre.

Initial word was that the gunmen were freelancers after the bounty on Coll's head. A consistent thread humming along the underworld grapevine was that the hammer was dropping from both the law and from Lucky Luciano. Lucky's edict—that the next one to make a hit without his approval would die—was on everyone's lips. No one—not the mob, not the cops—had a clue as to the current whereabouts of Mad Dog Coll, who was assumed by both factions to be holed up somewhere under a false identity. A police pick-up-on-sight APB on Coll had thus far yielded nothing.

As the meeting broke up, the team filing out of the squad room, one man lagged behind.

Devlin and Dave Heyer had been friends since before The Gangland Squad came into existence. They'd taken fire together on raids when hoodlums had resisted arrest. That sort of thing creates a strong bond when a man's survival depends on the ones covering his back, breeding a level of trust deeper than can be found in many marriages. Devlin had been best man at Dave's wedding and was godfather to the couple's child.

Heyer said, "Hell of a day."

"Got that right."

"Say, Tom, if you're not doing anything this weekend, Marla's off with the baby to visit her mother in Jersey."

With everything else crowding in on his day, this personal remark caught Devlin's attention. The service record of every man on the squad had been thoroughly vetted. Heyer and Devlin were the only two members whose number of citations was almost matched by the number disciplinary actions filed against them over the years. They were the only members of the unit who had been accused of being rogue cops for breaking so many rules, overlooked only because they always delivered satisfactory results.

"I hope there's no drama on the domestic front."

Heyer's lean, dark Semitic face broke into a grin.

"Not a chance. Love reigns supreme on the home front. Marla's mom gets lonely after her dad died. I was thinking maybe you and me could round up a poker game. Or take in the fights. Or both."

"Thanks, Dave. Why not?"

"Say, that was some business, you slapping down Vince Coll before the shooting started. In full view of everyone present like one of those two-fisted detective stories I'm always reading in the magazines. You're famous up and down the avenue now after what happened. Ten feet tall and bulletproof! The street rats will run for cover when they see you coming."

"Thanks, Dave. I hope you're right. I feel more like a guy walking around with a big fat target painted on his back."

A few minutes later, when Devlin reached the commissioner's office, Tuchman was facing a half-dozen noisy reporters shouting questions at him about the massacre. Tuchman caught Devlin's eye, and then curtailed the questioning, dismissing a roomful of grumbling newsmen with his assurance that every lead was being vigorously pursued.

He and Devlin watched the last of them file out. Then they stepped into Tuchman's private sanctum, a corner office dominated by the commissioner's enormous desk and a picture window that offered a panoramic view of Manhattan.

Tuchman asked, "Anything new since we spoke last?"

"We're on it but so far no, nothing."

"So Coll has again vanished from sight, holed up with that woman of his. That's two needles in one hell of a haystack."

"I should be out on the street with my man right now, tracking down leads. He's hot. He'll be running out of places to hide if he hasn't already."

"I may have a lead," said Tuchman. "It just came in unless it turns out to have been a crank call. Sounded real enough. Ever hear of Ralph Peer?"

"New to me."

"Same here. Says he makes those records people play on their Victrolas. Sounds like a successful businessman over the phone. So maybe he is."

"And he's got lead on Vince Coll?"

"That's what he implied when he got through to me. Says he's registered with a group of musicians at the Waldorf-Astoria."

"That's high class for musicians."

"That's what I mean. Could have been a crank call. But he asked for you by name. Very subtly slipped in that he's calling about, and I quote, 'the trouble down the street.' That speakeasy is just down the street from the Waldorf. Said he was choosing his words carefully in case someone at the hotel switchboard was listening in."

"Could be something there," said Devlin.

"My sentiments exactly. Get over to the Waldorf. See if this guy Peer has anything we can use."

"I'm on my way."

"And Devlin, if it does concern what happened today... Tuchman paused as if searching for the right words to express a troubling thought. He turned to stand before the plate glass window, his hands clasped behind his back, gazing out across the city. He said, "Those newshounds I just got rid of aren't the only ones dissatisfied with the way things stand. Damn Vince Coll. What I saw today at that speakeasy, all those bodies being carted away, the blood splattered everywhere, that's going to stay with me the rest of my life. I see it now every time I close my eyes. Things like this aren't supposed to happen in a civilized society. Dammit, it's our duty to see that something gets done about Coll."

"Gangsters in New York have become tolerated," said Devlin. "When they rub out each other, who cares? But that little boy last year and what happened today, innocent people slaughtered, no one wants a city like that."

Tuchman turned from the window. He perched on the corner of his desk

"Lucky has handed down his edict forbidding any killing not sanctioned by this board of mobsters he's created. With repeal just around the corner and the boys moving in to extort enterprise, they want to stop drawing attention to themselves. Dutch is smart enough to go along with the idea. But Coll, he's got everyone mad enough to kill him. Are you getting my drift, Tom?"

"Trying to, sir."

"Okay, here it is straight. No chaser, no sugar coating, and off the record. Say this Waldorf deal or some other lead develops that takes us to Coll. Something like that will happen, we both know it. And when it does, yes, we have something in common with Luciano and Schultz. We all want Vincent Coll out of the picture. Dead and gone."

"I'm still not catching the pitch, sir."

"Tom, I chose you to head up the Gangster Squad because you're honest, tenacious, tough...and you've got *imagination*. Hell, it was your idea to form an untouchable squad in the first place. So if, no, let's say *when*, you get your next chance at Coll, don't bother slapping him down in public or even arresting the kill-crazy son of a bitch. Use that imagination. Do whatever it takes to rub the guy out of the picture. That is when New York will start being safe again for its citizens."

"Imagination," said Devlin. "Got it."

"Again, this is off the record. But something has to be done, and frankly, Tom, you're the man to make that happen."

"Wouldn't have it any other way," said Devlin.

CHAPTER TWENTY-TWO

VINCE WAS FEELING great when he got back to the Cornish Arms. Killing always gave him a high, and often, like right now, it instilled in him an erotic impulse that made him want sex. Starting with Arn Fratelli, seemed like he'd been killing people all day. Killing had always fascinated and excited him.

There were the alley cats he and his brother Peter used to hunt down and torture when they were growing up. Before long he and Petey were rolling drunks, picking pockets for loose change after the rummies had passed out. If they found an old drunk who was only semi-conscious, the drunk might stir and grouse, but they never put up much of a struggle. Except for that time when an old wino, who they'd thought was passed out, came awake with a start and grabbed Petey by the throat. Without hesitation Vince had defended his brother by gripping hold of the old buzzard's scrawny throat and repeatedly smashing the back of his head into the alley pavement hard enough and long enough until the back of the drunk's skull cracked. His blood and brains were mush on the ground. That was the first man Vince killed.

In the years since, he'd sent plenty more to the graveyard

or to the bottom of the river wearing cement overshoes. The death of another by his hand often brought upon him the urge he was feeling now. Shoving his gun into Fritz's mouth and blasting away had paid the rat off. And it gave Vince an itch he had to scratch.

He would need to work some on Lottie. She only made herself available in that way when she damn well felt like it. She'd made it clear that the rest of the time it was hands off even though they were now husband and wife. Get her high, that was the ticket. Then maybe she'd let him have his way, and he could release the passion that had him so aroused.

When he stepped into their apartment, though, he could see at once, even before he'd had a chance to take off his hat and coat, that romance was not in the picture. She stood there in the center of the parlor. Fists clenched. A cold flame staring daggers from her eyes. Ready to scrap.

"Where the hell have you been?"

The curse was on her. After years of living together, he well knew the signs. She was pure poison when she got like this. One look, and he could tell she'd been into the reefer and the coke. With Lottie, that was like pouring gasoline on a fire.

Vince hung his coat and hat on the peg next to the door, still feeling good though he could tell he was in for a rough time. He was not in the habit of taking her guff.

"Where have I been? What the hell does it look like? I've been out. Shut up and go cut me a line."

Lottie growled a curse, adding, "I finished off the blow. The reefer too."

"Selfish bitch."

"I asked you where you've been."

"None of your business," said Vince. "What's it to you?"

"Vincent, we've been through this before."

"Sure we have. Every damn month."

"You're my man. I've got a right to know."

"Like hell you do. Now I've got to make a goddamn run uptown to score. So stop bugging me with questions." He glanced around their flat. "Where the hell is Trigger?"

"Don't change the subject, and don't you worry about Trigger. Worry about *me*, damn you."

Vince made a rude sound.

"Listen to the frail talk big. Stow it, chickie. I'm going back out. Where's Trigger?"

Her knees bent slightly. She gave the impression that she might be about to pounce.

"Who's the bimbo you're spending time with?"

Vince blinked, caught off guard.

"What?"

"You heard me. Big hero saves her precious music case."

"Someone's been talking."

"You were just out spending time with her now, weren't you, you cheating son of a bitch? I'll ask you one more time. Who is she?"

Vince said, "Well ain't you well informed. My business is my business. It ain't none of your business. I'll ask you one more time. Where do you get all this malarkey from?"

"Who is she, Vince?"

"I know who the rat is," said Vince. "I'll have a talk with Trigger."

"Who is she, Vince?"

Vince warned himself to calm down. Lottie remained in a crouch, poised as if to physically attack him. He was careful to maintain a safe distance between them. She practically had steam sprouting from her ears. Think practically, he told himself. The exultation he'd been riding was gone. So was his hard-on. A noisy spat could draw attention, leading to a neighbor's domestic disturbance call to the cops. Rotten timing for something like that to happen. He must keep Lottie calm. Don't let this blow up into a knock-down drag-out brawl. It wouldn't be their first. But that had to be avoided.

He said, softening the edge in his voice, "You've got me all wrong, Lottie. There's nothing like that going on. I'll bring Trigger by. He'll set you straight."

Lottie said, "I want the truth now, and I want it from you." The edge softened in her voice too, even when she added, "Who is she?"

"It was innocent, babe. Don't worry, I won't be seeing her again. She's been through enough. I don't want anything more happening to her."

"Well, you are one noble son of a bitch, aren't you, Vince?"

"Damn it, Lottie—"

"Relax. Nothing's going to happen to her. I just want to know. Tell Mama."

"Okay," said Vince. "It just happened, all right? One of those things. You know how it goes. We met after I stopped some punk from trying to make off with her music case. Ask your pet weasel Trigger next time you see him. He'll tell you truth."

"Sure he will. After you've had a talk with him. So you tell me, Vince. Who are we talking about?"

"Her name's Sara Carter. She's part of a group of musicians in from Tennessee. You got nothing to worry about. They're leaving town after they play a concert tonight at Carnegie Hall."

"Very classy. Thanks, Vinnie. That's all I wanted to know."

Lottie snagged her coat off the peg. Slipping into it, she grabbed her purse and stepped into the kitchenette.

Vince said, "Now what? You've got it all wrong, Lottie. She didn't do anything wrong and neither did I. It was just, I don't know, a change of pace to visit with her. That's all. She's just a simple, decent country woman."

"She's dead is what she is," said Lottie. "You louse, I know you. You just wanted to bang yourself a hillbilly...nless you already have."

"Not so loud, baby. The neighbors—"

"The hell with the neighbors. And the hell with you."

She yanked open a drawer next to the sink and withdrew the icepick. Concealing the icepick in her purse. Vince positioned himself between her and the door.

"Where the hell do you think you're going?"

"Get out of my way. I'm going to make an example of your hillbilly bitch so word gets around not to poach what's mine."

He grabbed her by the arm.

"Stop it, you stupid frail. Only a dumb broad would talk to me like that. You're not going anywhere."

"Sez you."

She brought up a knee hard and fast into his groin. Vince grunted like a wounded beast. He jack-knifed to the floor at her feet, drawing in upon himself, blind to everything except the incredible pain exploding within him. The only sound to pierce his agony was the sound of the door closing behind Lottie as she stormed out.

CHAPTER TWENTY-THREE

WHEN DUTCH SCHULTZ was shown into the library of Lucky Luciano's penthouse, Lucky did not rise to greet him from the plush armchair in which he sat, sipping from a long-stemmed glass of red wine. Nor did he offer Dutch a glass of wine. Dutch didn't mind. He was just glad to be on speaking terms with Lucky Luciano since, over the past year or so, the alternative had proven fatal for any number of guys.

Lucky was smooth as silk these days, but that didn't fool Dutch. At thirty years of age, sitting there in his richly brocaded smoking jacket, the slim Italian-born Boss of New York, well-groomed and composed, could have passed for a leading man in the movies except for the old knife scar down his cheek that marred his matinee idol features.

"You took your time getting here, Dutch."

Shultz realized with a shock that he was standing before Lucky with his hat in his hands like some damn underling. It was too late to do anything about that without drawing attention to the fact.

"Had to round up a gun crew for the drive over," he said. "They're outside hobnobbing with your boys."

The past eighteen months had seen a gang war engulf New York. By the time the smoke cleared, everything had changed. A changing of the guard, nothing less.

The aging, traditional mafia bosses who had started their criminal careers in Italy, the so-called "Mustache Petes," had lived their lives upholding the "Old World Mafia" principles of honor, tradition, respect, and dignity. They refused to work with non-Italians, were even skeptical of working with non-Sicilians. Many of the old guard would only work with men from their own village in Sicily. The younger generation like Dutch and Lucky had chafed at this conservatism that kept the young bloods locked in place as poor street-level thugs. Their generation was willing to work with Jewish and Irish gangsters as long as there was money to be made. Lucky began cultivating ties with other young mobsters. This led to a revolt against the Mustache Petes, and that led to war.

They called him Lucky because he'd survived so many attempts on his life, the toughest, most devious, most ruthless and power-hungry upstart of them all. The old-timers were rubbed out to a man ,and Lucky's vision took form: a crime syndicate in which the Italian, Jewish, and Irish gangs pooled their resources, organizing crime into a lucrative business. Lucky rose to become New York's dominant crime boss so fast it had seemed to Dutch like it happened overnight.

Having attained the pinnacle of the city's underworld, Lucky these days was setting policies and directing criminal enterprises along with a handful of other mafia bosses who had divided the city among themselves. Lucky's "crime family" controlled illegal gambling, extortion, and prostitution. He also controlled construction, trucking, and garbage hauling businesses throughout the city and lately had become involved in labor union activities.

Lucky set aside his empty wine glass and regarded Schultz from above pyramided fingers.

"Ever get the idea, Dutch, that people weren't listening to what you say?"

Dutch wasn't sure how to respond. He shrugged.

"Guess so."

"I put out the word for everyone to hold off on the killing, and what happens?"

"Someone ain't listening," said Dutch. "But it ain't me, Lucky. You know that, right? It's why I need a full contingent of bodyguards just for a crosstown drive. It's that damn Mad Dog. I've been keeping my head down, running my business, and that's it."

"I know that's what you're doing, Dutch."

"You do?"

"I got a couple boys planted in your mob. They keep an eye on you and let me know what's up."

"Uh, okay."

"You hear about what happened this afternoon?"

"Couple of guys tried to hit Coll in a speak. Yeah, I heard."

"It'll be splashed all over the early editions," said Lucky. "It'll give those reform clowns more ammunition to come after us. I tell everyone to lay off on the rough stuff and now this. Innocent bystanders caught in the line of fire. Dutch, I remember you walking into that Bronx police station and offering a house in Westchester to the cop who gunned down Vince Coll. So I have to ask. What happened today, were those your guys?"

"Hell no, Lucky. I had absolutely nothing to do with it. I told you—"

"Relax. I heard what you told me. I just want to hear it from you when we're face to face, eye to eye. Those two punks were freelancers. With all the hate against Coll, they must've figured if they hit him, it would pay off. It did, but not the way they figured it."

"That damn Coll. If it's not coming from him, it's coming at him. Hell, what about what happened last week?"

Five gunmen had invaded a Bronx apartment where Coll was rumored to frequent. They opened fire with pistols and submachine guns. Three Coll gangsters and a female bystander were killed, three others wounded. Coll didn't show up until thirty minutes after the shooting.

Lucky said, "And so you have no idea where Coll is? I wouldn't want you holding out on me so you could nail him yourself, Dutch."

"Lucky, I'm being straight with you on this all the way. But I'll tell you what. If we could pin that rat down, I'd be the man to drop the hammer on him. You know that, right? I'll cancel his check and make sure it got done right."

"Just do nothing 'til you hear from me." Lucky lifted an index finger to emphasize the point. "I've had a private detective agency track down Coll and his woman. He couldn't stay hidden forever. We're an organization now, Dutch, and you're a part of it. We're laying down a template that will carry us for generations."

"Template?"

"I'm the boss of bosses," said Lucky, "but from here on out we're in alliance with the other New York mobs. It's been agreed that any hit has to be sanctioned by the ruling board of directors. That's me and the other bosses. Everything's going to be jake, like running a legit operation. By the numbers. No exceptions. That will prevent gang wars. We can get every mob in the country to join up. Organize. That's the future."

"So, uh, how does Coll fit into that?"

"The other bosses buy that he's too far out of line. But some of them have worked deals with Coll over the years. They want absolute proof that he's made one hit too many. I don't like it, but I went along with that. It's been a hard road just getting these boys to bury the hatchet and get this far.

We just made the final handshake yesterday, but frankly, it's a damn fragile alliance at this early stage. But as for Coll, one more misstep, and he's done. Then we go ahead with a hit only if there's no other recourse."

"What does that mean? You can't reason with that crazy punk. No one can"

"It means we only hit the punk with full approval of the board *if* he crosses the line one more time. That's how new this all is. We're making sure to set a precedent."

"Even after a day like today?"

"We've got to keep things on the up and up for any of this to work," said Lucky. "We're establishing a precedent for when future situations like this arise." He sipped from his glass of wine. "There has been a break in the case, as our police friends would say."

"Is that so?"

"With as many connections as we've got up and down the avenue in addition to the cops," said Lucky, "it had to happen, and it did."

"So we know where the bugger's holed up? When do I kill our mad dog?"

"Shouldn't be long," said Lucky. "From here on out, Coll screws up, and he's a dead man."

CHAPTER TWENTY-FOUR

WHEN TOM DEVLIN was introduced to Sara Carter upon his arrival at the Waldorf-Astoria, his first thought was, *well, well, well. The mystery woman has been found.* He concealed his surprise. She appeared considerably worse for the wear, seated beside another woman near a window.

Ralph Peer had worn a cautious expression when he opened the door to Devlin's knock. Sharply attired, he exuded a crisp air of command though it was clear that he was a man with much on his mind.

Devlin flashed his badge, identifying himself.

"Someone here called Commissioner Tuchman. The commissioner sent me."

"I made the call, Detective. Please come in."

Sara Carter sat with her hands clasped in her lap. When Peer introduced them, her eyes met Devlin's for only the fraction of a second. She lowered those vacant eyes, conveying the impression of someone lost within herself.

The woman next to Sara was introduced as Maybelle. A stern-faced customer standing beside the writing desk was introduced as AP Carter, Sara's husband. Devlin hadn't seen Sara's wedding ring in the dim lighting of the speakeasy. He saw it now. The three of them were well turned out, yet their appearance and informal manner said country. They each exchanged a nod with Devlin upon being introduced. No handshakes.

"The Carter Family from Tennessee," said Peer, a glow of prideful hyperbole warming his words. "They and another recording artist of mine, Mr. Jimmie Rodgers, whom you will meet shortly, will be performing in a few hours at Carnegie Hall."

If that was intended to impress Devlin, it succeeded.

He said, "Sorry you had to call the cops. I was told this has something to do with Vincent Coll?"

Peer cleared his throat.

"Yes, well, I'll ask you to step across the hallway with me, Detective. There's something, er, someone I want you to see." He added, "Won't you come with us, AP?"

AP grumbled something to himself that no one could hear before saying, "Very well." He left with Peer and Devlin. When the door closed behind them, Sara emitted a sigh of relief.

"I never thought they'd leave."

Maybelle drew a glass of water from the bathroom sink.

"Here, honey. You've got to get yourself together. We've got a concert coming up in a few hours. It won't be easy, but for now we've got to put everything else on hold."

Sara declined the glass of water with a shake of her head.

"Remember when we first set eyes on Vincent? The boy who tried to steal my autoharp...it wasn't respect he was showing Vince when he returned the autoharp to me and fled. It was fear. He knew something we didn't know. He knew who Mad Dog Vince Coll was."

Maybelle said, "It's okay, hon. You've told me what happened. We can talk about it some more later. I'm sure we will. But right now—"

"Maybelle, I saw him kill a man. The poor devil was on

his knees begging for his life and Vincent, he just…he just… oh, Maybelle. And now they're saying maybe he sent that man who tried to kill me with a knife. How could I have been so wrong? Am I going crazy?"

"We came all this way to do a job," Maybelle reminded her, softening her voice, trying to generate enthusiasm in Sara and in herself. "We have to get our minds on tonight. We have to freshen up, dear. I know you must be exhausted but—"

Sara's eyes popped wide open.

"Funny thing, Maybelle. I'm not tired at all. Oh, maybe a little worn down from all that's happened, but mostly I'm just God-blessed flat-out *angry*."

"Angry?"

"I'm mad at everyone including myself. Especially myself for letting everything that's been pushing me drive me crazy."

"Reckon you've got a right at that."

"Reckon I have. It's like the words we sing to "Amazing Grace." I've been blind for a long time, Maybelle. Too doggone long. But now I sur ''nuff can see, like a veil's been lifted from before my eyes. I'm mad at AP for what he done, deserting me and our children so I'd be driven to another man just to survive. I'm mad at Mr. Peer for dragging us up here to this big cold New York town. And I'm durn tootin' mad at that Vince Coll. Dang, was I snookered. He just wanted his way with a dumb country girl in between killing people."

"Someday soon someone's going to kill him, and the world will be a better place," said Maybelle. "But right now I just want the world to stop going crazy until we play this concert."

"I've never been a violent person, Maybelle."

"I know that. You know how much you mean to me. You're a virtuous woman with a good heart."

"But damn," said Sara. "I'm mad. I've built me up a head of steam, and I don't know what to do with it. I feel like punching someone on the jaw, starting with the people I just got through naming."

"Except for yourself, of course," ventured Maybelle with a straight face. "Imagine playing Carnegie Hall with a black eye and a busted jaw. Mr. Peer would certainly not approve."

The laugh they shared seemed to drain the moment of its tension.

Sara said, "You're right as always, May. But can I show you something?"

"Of course, hon. What is it?"

Sara undid the top two buttons of her frock so she could slide her fingers inside. She withdrew a small photograph. She handed it to Maybelle, a photo of Coy Bays. A handsome, bronze hillbilly god looking healthy in the Tennessee sun.

Sara said, "When I went out with Vince...honestly, in my heart I was cheating on Coy more than I was cheating on AP. Maybelle, I keep that picture pressed against my heart at all times. And I always will."

"Enough," said Maybelle. "Sara, please. The concert tonight is the only thing that matters"

Sara returned the photograph to where it came from. Her eyes were no longer vacant.

She said, "So what are we waiting for?"

CHAPTER TWENTY-FIVE

TRIGGER APPEARED to be a young man asleep, catching a nap on the closet floor. He lay on his side. Knees slightly bent. A flask in his hand. A trace of vomit mixed with blood snaked from the corner of his half-open mouth.

Devlin knelt on one knee. He checked a limp wrist for a pulse beat. Finding none, he thumbed open one of Trigger's closed eyelids. Then he rose to face the men who stood observing him with expectant curiosity.

"Stone cold dead."

Peer briefed Devlin after Jimmie opened the locked door to allow them in. Peer filled Devlin in on the situation while Devlin formed an impression of each man. Jimmie Rodgers and AP Carter were contrasting personalities yet shared a rustic, downhome demeanor. They clearly regarded Peer as their social superior, and Peer did embody a clever urban sophistication.

Rodgers said, "Well, dang."

Peer said, "What in the world could have happened to him?"

AP muttered, "It's the Lord's work. The heathen tried to

murder Sara. He's paid for that transgression. God's sword is swift."

Devlin picked up the flask and gave it a few shakes. Empty. Holding the flask to his nostrils, he sniffed, causing him to wince.

"Where'd he get this?"

Jimmie said, "I gave it to him. Bought it off a bootlegger at the train station when I first hit town. Told me it was moonshine. I gave it to the boy to quiet him down."

Devlin tossed the flask onto the body.

"It did that. That 'legger sold you a flask of wood alcohol."

New York was experiencing an epidemic, along the Bowery and Skid Row, of deaths resulting from the consumption of wood alcohol. For years, much of the industrial alcohol in the United States had been poisoned under order of the US government. The government created this deadly blend to discourage criminals from hijacking industrial alcohol and selling it to the public. The blend included a fatal amount of methyl (wood) alcohol. This policy failed to end the hijacking and distribution of such alcohol, and its consumption.

"Hoo-wee," said Jimmie. "Reckon that was Trigger's bad luck and my good luck."

Peer said, "What are we going to do about this, Detective?"

Devlin turned toward the telephone on the room's writing desk.

"I need to make a call."

"Is that wise?" asked Peer. "What if someone on the hotel switch board listens in?"

"What if they do? They'll want this body out of here much as we do. And that's what I'm about to set in motion. I'm just keeping things off the record. That is, unless you'd prefer reporting this to the house detective."

"Goodness, no," said Peer without hesitation. "I appreciate you taking a hand in this, Devlin. You're quite right. Yes, the matter requires alacrity and, naturally, discretion. It's what I was hoping for when I called the commissioner. We must avoid publicity at all cost."

"We will. I've got an idea."

"Idea?"

"We can make this work for both of us. I'm about to knock off two birds with one stone."

Devlin dialed the switchboard. He requested one of the few telephone numbers he knew by heart.

Dave Heyer picked up on the third ring. A baby's squalling carried loud enough across the connection for Devlin to practically see Dave holding an armful of squalling baby while answering the phone. The baby sounds subsided somewhat so he must have handed his armful over to the missus when he heard Devlin's voice.

"What's up, skipper?"

"Something you'll want a piece of if I'm not mistaken." Devlin gave him the room number. "Flag yourself over here fast as you can, Dave. And call Doc Hoffman. I want him to drop whatever he's doing and get over here with a full rig."

"Ah ha. Freight elevator, I assume."

"You assume right. Uh, by the way, we don't happen to have a telephone number for our friend Lucky."

"Not if it's the Lucky I think you're thinking of."

"How about Winchell?"

"Winchell? As in Walter?"

"Uh huh."

"Sorry, skip. Two strikes, and you're out."

"Make it over here, Dave, fast as you can."

"See you there," said Dave, and he broke the connection.

Devlin hung up the phone. He turned to face the three men.

"I've set something in play." He indicated the corpse. "This will be dealt with quietly. No publicity."

Peer was dry washing his hands.

"But who were you talking to just now? And you mentioned a doctor."

"I was speaking to another police officer if that makes you feel better. Dr. Hoffman is a licensed practitioner whom I've worked with before. His complete discretion can be counted on."

"Well, that sounds fine certainly. But I would prefer some detail as to what you have in mind."

Devlin placed a hand on the businessman's shoulder and looked him straight in the eye.

"Peer, I was sent here to get you out of a mess. If you're placing this matter in my hands, you're going to have to have faith in what I'm up to. The less you know, the better off you are."

Peer considered this with a harrumph. He didn't like being addressed without a "mister" before his name. He consulted a gold-plated pocket watch. He spoke to Jimmie and AP.

"Gentlemen, if Detective Devlin has no objection, it's past time, I'm sure, for all of us to make final preparations for the concert. I've arranged transportation. We shall depart on schedule. The show must go on."

"The show must go on," Jimmie repeated. "But I do got one question. Detective, you were just now asking your pal about a phone number for Winchell. Would that be the radio feller you was talking 'bout?"

"It would be."

Peer interjected, "Walter Winchell is attending the concert. We bought advertising on his show."

"You know him?"

"Uh no, not exactly. I don't know him personally. All communication was handled through his agent until we met today when he showed up at a rehearsal to gather background for when he writes a review."

Jimmie said, "When I had the man's ear, he told me to call him if I ever had something he could use."

Peer harrumphed again.

"It's called gossip."

Jimmie reached into a breast pocket for his wallet, from which he extracted Walter Winchell's card. He handed the card to Devlin, who jotted the phone number down on a pad on the writing desk before handing the card back to Jimmie.

"Thanks. This is going to come in handy."

The business card went back into the wallet. The wallet went back into the breast pocket.

"Shucks," said Jimmie, "I'm just glad to help out."

"Then you gents can be on your way, and thanks for your cooperation. The important thing for everyone to keep in mind is that no bad publicity is a two-way street. In that I mean everything—everything—about this stays strictly undercover for everyone involved, okay? None of this ever happened. Not the assault on Mrs. Carter, none of it. Understood?"

"Most certainly," said Peer.

"You got my vote," said Jimmie. "My lips are sealed." He gave them a wink. "That is, until I start to singing."

AP grunted a monosyllable.

Peer said to AP and Jimmie, "Very well then. We'll gather in the lobby at departure time. And thank you again, Jimmie, for your help in this matter."

Another grunt from AP.

Jimmie said, "Sure 'nuff, Mr. Peer. But I don't mind telling you I sure am glad that from here on out, it's just me and my guitar. Rough stuff and all them guns makes a poor boy like me kind of nervous."

"Why Jimmie, you're no stranger to rough stuff. You carry a gun."

"My little pea shooter? Pshaw, that's show biz, Mr. Peer. It ain't even loaded! It keeps a lid on when things get heated, folks know I'm packing. But truth is, Jimmie Rodgers does his best to stay *out* of trouble, yes sir."

Peer showed them out.

When he returned, Devlin was again on one knee next to the body in the closet. He'd gathered up Trigger's pair of pistols. He used his personal kerchief to wipe both guns clean of fingerprints before returning a .45 to the shoulder holster under each of Trigger's arms.

Peer said, "I want you to know, Detective, how much I appreciate your efforts on our behalf. Needless to say, I hardly anticipated anything like this occurring. May I offer a financial contribution as a token of my gratitude? What might be a suitable sum, if you don't mind my asking."

"No need to ask," said Devlin. "There aren't many cops in this town who aren't for sale, but I'm one of them. Keep your money, Mr. Peer. What I've got in mind will bring me its own payoff."

"I meant no disrespect, of course, offering you money the way I did. I'm used to business shenanigans. But I'm rather new at crime."

"Crime? What crime? Our friend Trigger here is dead by his own hand from drinking bad hooch. So you had a small part in relocating a dead body. So what? This is New York. You read the papers. You know what goes on in this city day in and day out. Okay, call your part in this a crime if it makes you feel better, but trust me, no one cares. Neither should you. You've got a big night planned. That's your job. I'll take this from here."

"Well," said Peer, "I can hardly turn down an offer like that. Thank you, Devlin. But before I let myself out, are you sure you can't at least offer me just a clue as to what the devil you have in mind?"

"Well, if you insist," said Devlin. "I intend to frame Vince Coll for Trigger's murder."

CHAPTER TWENTY-SIX

WALTER WINCHELL LEANED back in his chair. He fired up a cigarette. Squinting through the smoke, he read the words he'd just typed.

Five planes brought dozens of machine gats from Chicago Friday. Local banditti have made one hotel a virtual arsenal, and several hot spots are ditto because Master Coll is giving them the headache.

Yes. That would do. Hardly literary prose, but it's what millions of readers expected from "Mrs. Winchell's little boy," as he often referred to himself in print and on his radio show. Slangy, colloquial as hell, this was the final paragraph of his latest *On Broadway* column, now ready for *The Daily Mirror's* bulldog edition. A bike messenger, posted on 24-hour standby, would have it crosstown on the editor's desk in no time.

He stepped outside and handed the bike messenger the manila envelope containing the manuscript. The boy slid the envelope into his bag and pedaled off.

The speakeasy massacre had elevated Mad Dog Coll into hot news once again. So what would happen next? The influx of imported hit men, most of them registered (along with their artillery) at the Forrest Hotel, made it clear that whatever happened next would not go well for Coll who'd gone undercover, hid out with his woman somewhere in the city under assumed names. Easy enough since most of their newspaper photos were snapped at court appearances where Coll and his moll had kept their faces partially covered or averted from the camera.

Winchell glanced at his wristwatch. Right on schedule. Time for dinner. He decided on the Stork Club. As the man with his finger on the pulse of Broadway, Walter Winchell frequented only the best. Up and down the Great White Way, his meals and drinks were always on the house. Tonight after dinner he would catch Ralph Peer's show at Carnegie Hall starring his hillbilly performers.

Who could tell where Peer's musical vision might lead? The man had become successful from the recording and marketing the music of Negroes. Could that success be repeated with this country music played and sung by people like the Carters and Jimmie Rodgers? Peer envisioned a future of folks of both races listening to their favorite music at home over the radio or in public places like dance halls and taverns, made possible thanks to the revolutionary concept of mass marketing the music manufactured on plastic discs.

The average consumer considered records a luxury. The Victrola, on which such records were played, was an expensive item sold in furniture stores, allowing only a privileged few the pleasure of opera and classical music in one's own home. But if records were to be mass produced, delivering popular music of all styles to the public, the sky was the limit. Tonight's show would be the first real indicator of big things to come or an ill-conceived flop.

And Walter Winchell would be there.

He went about preparing for an evening out. His houseboy had already spread his clothes out upon the bed. Stylish yet nondescript, personally tailored to present his slight, wiry frame to the world as slim, energetic. As toast of the Great White Way, he never stepped out without looking the part.

Though he hailed from a poor Jewish neighborhood in Harlem, Broadway had been in his blood since youth. Dropping out of school in the sixth grade, he began performing as a dancer in vaudeville. His career in journalism started with the posting of notes about his vaudeville troop on backstage bulletin boards. Hired onto the *Vaudeville News* in 1920, he'd gone on to catch the rising star of radio. Becoming in a dozen years the top syndicated columnist in America, his weekly radio show was broadcast throughout the world.

After his bath and fully clothed, Winchell admired his reflection in a full length mirror, observing nothing to displease him. The telephone rang. He answered.

A man's voice said, "Am I speaking to Walter Winchell?"

Authoritative and commanding. Not a tone Winchell cared for unless he himself was using it.

"This is Winchell."

"Detective Thomas Devlin."

Should have known, thought Winchell.

"Yes, Detective?"

He kept his tone tentative, not wanting to give away too much. The gossip he peddled in the newspapers and over the radio came from an endless variety of sources—waiters, dishwashers and chauffeurs to show business bigshots and gangsters, some cultivated under the guise of friendship. He often engaged Ed Sullivan in amiable conversation, running with newsworthy tidbits before the inexperienced little weasel realized their importance. Informants were embedded among the ranks of law enforcement. This Devlin could be such a cop, calling with a piece of usable information. He'd lined up so many contacts in the department, it was hard to remember every name.

Devlin said, "I'm calling because I want information."

"Is that right?"

"I need a phone number."

"How do I know you, Detective?"

"You don't. You don't want to."

"I can believe that. What's this about?"

"I need Lucky Luciano's telephone number."

Winchell couldn't hold back a snort of laughter.

"And why would I have Lucky Luciano's phone number?"

"Why wouldn't you? Talk is you've got the inside line to anyone who matters in this town."

"Detective, you've have ten seconds. Now would be a good time to say something that will keep me from hanging up."

Devlin said, "You think you're safe in your ivory tower, don't you?"

"That's not good enough. Goodbye, Detective."

"Don't hang up," said Devlin. "I can make your life nothing but hell if I want to, Mr. Broadway, and I will unless I get what I want."

"Give it your best try. You and I are done."

"I know what you've been up to," said Devlin. "A word to the wise, Walter. Cooperate with me. I know what you've been up to, and I know how to use it against you. And you don't have to guess much to know what I'm talking about. Do you, newsman? Now give me the goddamn number, or I'll do the hanging up and the next time we talk it will be in a court of law."

Winchell gave him the number; a number he'd long ago committed to memory.

He said, "I trust you will keep confidential where you got that number. Mr. Luciano is a personal acquaintance. I don't wish to cause him trouble or embarrassment."

"Those guys like that make trouble for themselves," said Devlin, "Thank you for your help, citizen."

"Uh, Detective. Could you spare a moment? Long as we're not at each other's throat, I do have an offer for you to consider."

"Let's hear it."

"I like your style. How about a monthly payout—in cash, of course—as reimbursement for passing along to me any newsworthy tidbits concerning public figures that I could use—"

"You mean dirt."

A click in Winchell's ear, followed by the dial tone. He pronged the telephone's earpiece.

He said to himself, "Win some, lose some."

Devlin sounded like he knew his onions. It was worth giving out Lucky's phone number to stay on the good side of a cop like this Devlin with his claim of knowing what Winchell was "up to." What the hell could that mean? Or was it a bluff?

Hell, thought Winchell, I'm always "up to" something! It came with his role as a sort of halfway house between the law and the criminal element. Information was his bread and butter gathered from cops feeding him dope on criminals and from criminals tipping him off to the doings of the police. His life included a wide range of characters from murderous gangsters to show people. Things always got dicey when those two worlds collided.

CHAPTER TWENTY-SEVEN

AP CARTER and Jimmie Rodgers stood in the lobby of the Waldorf-Astoria, near the front main entrance, waiting for the others. Their instruments were at Carnegie Hall along with, at last report, a sold out house. New York nightlife was already underway. A constant flow of human activity swirled about the vast lobby.

AP, occupied with worry, noted little of it. He couldn't remember ever feeling this tied up inside. Even the rounder Jimmie Rodgers was calling tonight's concert "the big gig," and in fact, it was the biggest, most important concert of AP's life. From this point on tonight, it was vitally important that nothing—absolutely nothing—go wrong. This was not the first time the Carter Family had played to a city audience, but it was the first time they would hit the stage with this much riding on a single performance.

His dream from the beginning had been to take mountain music to a wider popular audience. Faith in the dream kept him going. The dream never died. But tonight newspaper critics would be in the audience along with radio personalities like Walter Winchell. His dreams were coming true. But always, it seemed, with a sour note. The dream had sent him into the hills last winter, foraging for new song material, neglecting his husbandly duties. What was a man supposed to do when driven by a dream? He was still paying for that.

Leave it to Sara to get involved with a New York gangster, a massacre, and an attempt on her life. Talk about complications! But there was no way they could turn back now or put any of this on hold to be dealt with at some future time.

Jimmie said, "Here they come."

Sara and Maybelle were wearing their best. They blended in well here in this big city hotel among the expensively tailored upper crust. Then a nip of irritation bit him when he saw how happy and contented Sara appeared to be. The two of them looked downright cheerful as they advanced arm-in-arm, Maybelle saying something that brought a chuckle, brightening Sara's features. A short time ago she'd been distraught, in shock from all that had occurred. And here she was, her regal beauty alive, seemingly carefree.

Everything else blurred into insignificance when AP saw her coming toward him, the way it always had. He wished there was some way he could undo the past. Looking back, yes, he should have stayed home with Sara and the children, caring and providing for them during the winter rather than traipsing about the hills, tracking down songs. But even such an admission had done nothing to mend the break between them.

The P in AP's middle name stood for Pleasant. Alvin Pleasant Delaney Carter. He'd often wondered how it came to be that, born with a name like that, he'd grown up to become such a dour, gruff personality. AP often wished for the patience to abide those things that troubled him, which were many. But that hadn't happened yet and likely never would.

Jimmie bowed gallantly and smiled with a wink when the women reached them.

"My, my, don't you ladies sure 'nuff add some class to these here proceedings."

They each smiled a polite thank you. AP lightly touched Sara's elbow.

"Wife, I'd like a word with you."

Sara frowned but did not resist. She and AP stepped to the side, beyond earshot of Maybelle and Jimmie who were engaged in conversation. Sara reclaimed her elbow from AP's touch.

"Yes, what is it?"

"Well, it's just that tonight is a mighty serious occasion. And here you are, acting all gay and frivolous."

"Acting, yes," she said. "And what's wrong with that? Am I supposed to look like I'm just back from a funeral? It's show business, AP. I want people to think I'm having a wonderful time."

"But are you? Having a good time, I mean."

"AP, what the heck has got into you? Stage fright at your age?"

"What's got into *me*? That's something, coming from you after a day like today, spent getting yourself into a world of misery with a mad dog hoodlum. Shoot, I even seen you making eyes at cop, Devlin. Dang it all, what the blue blazes is going on with *you*? You're the one taking leave of your senses!"

AP took a step back when he saw the anger flare in Sara's eyes, her fists clenching as if she wanted to—as if she *needed* to!—take a swing at him.

Then she said in a quiet, deliberate voice, "AP, I'm staying with you and keeping this quiet. I want to hold our family together so our children will have the best upbringing we can give them. I want to keep this dog and pony show of yours on the road. But mister, get this straight. You and me are *done*. Got that or do you need it in writing? We're finished. Done with. It's over, AP. I don't love you anymore.

Don't you ever touch me when we're alone. And please don't make me repeat these words to you ever again. Do you hear what I'm saying?"

She didn't wait for an answer. She walked away. Observing this, Maybelle said something to Jimmie and went over to join Sara. AP rejoined Jimmie, who met him with a sympathetic smile.

"Domestic trouble?"

AP said, "Wish I was back in Tennessee."

Jimmie nodded.

"Womenfolk can get pent-up and easily riled when something big comes along." He mildly nudged AP with an elbow. "How 'bout you, hoss? Got yourself a case of the jitters? Stage fright?"

"That's what Sara just said. Reckon I'm doing all right. I could do without this gangster business she gotten us mixed up in. Up in the hills a man knows where he stands. Here in this dang city, some joker will shoot you down for no dang reason at all seems like. Life is a whole lot safer back home in Tennessee."

While AP's eyes stayed on Sara and Maybelle, chatting away beyond earshot, Jimmie studied AP.

"Say, old-timer. Tell me that story."

"What story?"

"The one about your mother. Mollie?"

"That was her name."

"A week after you was born, wasn't it? You told me once, I can't remember when. About the panther."

"Now what the blazes has that got to do with—"

"Aw go on, AP. We got nothing better to do, waitin' on Mr. Peer."

AP had never cared much for idle conversation, much less reciting an old family story. His thoughts and conversation was music-making, arranging songs, and such. But at this moment with folks passing by, hurrying and chatting among themselves in every direction, Jimmie stood leaning in. Persistent. Expectant. AP growled deep in his throat.

He said, "Ma wasn't but nineteen. Pa was out and about somewhere that night. Reckon I come from long line of ramblin' men. Home at that time was nothing but a one-room log cabin on Pine Ridge back there in Poor Valley. It was middle of the night. Ma was still in her day clothes. On her lap was me and the shotgun she was holding. She'd spotted a panther skulking around the property. Weren't no glass in the windows. Ma had put sack-cloth over 'em to keep out the wind. But that wouldn't keep out no panther. So that's how Mama sat up all that night, wide awake and alert in defense of me, her newborn. There." AP glared at Jimmie. "Heard enough?"

"Sure did," said Jimmie. "That's a mighty fine story, AP. You come from strong stock. So don't go telling me how peachy keen everything is down home where there's no paved streets, no electricity, no law for miles around, and they're just getting used to indoor plumbing. Ain't no place in this world that's more safe than another. Shoot. It's a dangerous world, hoss, no matter where you go."

"Reckon that's so," said AP. "Don't mean I have to like it."

"Showtime," said Jimmie.

He'd spotted Ralph Peer advancing through the flow of people. Sara and Maybelle returned to stand with Jimmie and AP. Peer was beaming. If he sensed any discord, he gave no indication.

"Aha, our little group has assembled! Very good!" He gestured expansively to the front entrance and the street scene beyond. "Let us be gone, people. On to Carnegie Hall and victory. Our chariot—that is to say our limousine—awaits."

CHAPTER TWENTY-EIGHT

NOT MANY YEARS AGO, Dr. Leland Hoffman had served at the pinnacle of New York's medical establishment. His downfall began with a botched illegal abortion performed on the daughter of a prominent politico. The stock market crash of '29 wiped out the politico but not before he managed to blacklist the doc in high society. Thereafter alcoholism, divorce, and a series of bad choices in life plagued the once prominent physician. Bounced from the medical profession, Hoffman managed to retain a semblance of dignity and respect finding work in the shadowy, smoke and mirrors world of gangland, tending to the injuries of hoods wounded by the police or in gang wars while at the same time, for a variety of reasons, occasionally cooperating with, and sometimes assisting, the police.

Not a healthy, easy life, and it showed.

At fifty-two, Hoffman could have easily passed for a man past seventy. His features sagged under an unruly thatch of thinning gray hair. The eyes held a permanent glaze. He had a drinker's nose. His appearance, while respectable enough, exuded the faint aroma of cheap pipe tobacco.

The doc arrived with Dave Heyer sooner than Devlin

expected, both men outfitted in medical white. Hoffman led the way, armed with a black medical bag and an air of professional authority. Close up, his were the saddest eyes Devlin had ever seen. Trigger's body remained sprawled in the open closet. Dave, wearing a visored cap, manning a gurney, entered in Hoffman's wake.

"How'd it go?" Devlin asked.

"Piece of cake," said Dave. "The hotel was glad to let us use the freight elevator."

"Sure they were. They'd have insisted if we hadn't asked. A stiff being wheeled out through the lobby? Bad form and lousy publicity for a fancy dump like this. Thanks for helping us out, Doc."

Hoffman indicated the body.

"Is that what I'm helping with? I daresay the fellow appears beyond any assistance I might provide."

"Not when it comes to getting him the hell out of here."

"Aha."

"We'll get him on this stretcher. Cover him up with a sheet. We take the stiff down the way you came up. No one's going to question or impede a physician overseeing the removal of a cadaver. The hotel's glad to see us go."

"And what if hotel management reports this man's death to the police?"

Dave pointed out, "Well, there is the fact that we are the police."

"Very well then," said Hoffman. "There remains only the matter of my fee."

"Now, Doc," said Dave. "We talked about that on the drive over." He added for Devlin's benefit, "I explained to Dr. Hoffman that this would have to go on his tab due to us needing him on such short notice."

Devlin added, "Doc, we don't carry payoff cash around in our back pockets."

"Well perhaps you should." The snip in his voice was

leavened by a noticeable slurring of the words. "Surely you gentlemen understand the problem with delayed payment. Is there no way we can—"

"You've trusted us before, Doc. "Trust us now."

"But surely a small advance—"

"Doc, you engage in criminal activity on a daily basis. And as Dave points out, he and I are the police. Doc, you can't negotiate with us. You have nothing to negotiate with. So stow it, okay? You're here so let's get on with it."

Hoffman stared down his heavily-veined nose at Devlin.

"You needn't be quite so candid. Very well. If I am assured by you that financial recompense is forthcoming, yes, let us proceed."

Devlin and Dave went about removing Trigger's remains from the closet. Rigor mortis had yet to set in. The body was cool but pliable. They placed it upon the gurney with little difficulty. Once it was on the gurney, Hoffman strapped the remains to the stretcher with professional skill and expediency.

Dave said, "Care to tell us the plan?"

Before Devlin could reply, Hoffman looked up from completing his inspection of the connections securing the body to the gurney.

"Gentlemen, please. I am here to perform a service. I do not wish to hear any discussion of illegal activity."

Dave said. "That's rich coming from you, Doc."

"I must insist."

Devlin said, "It's okay, Doctor. Get us out of this hotel, and you'll be on your way. Mum's the word, Dave. The less Doc knows about our business, the better."

"Right," said Dave.

"So let's do it."

Devlin walked across to the hotel room door, opened it and sent a glance in either direction up. A man and woman were entering their room several doors down. Devlin waited until their door closed, then he gave a nod. Dave, as medical assistant, proceeded to steer the gurney through the doorway with Doctor Hoffman in attendance, his little black bag and officious manner presenting exactly the effect Devlin wanted.

They proceeded along the corridor, Devlin looking for all the world like a man (a hotel employee, no doubt) accompanying two medicos discreetly removing some poor soul whose time had come. They passed a cluster of hotel guests who stood waiting for an elevator, tuxedoed gentlemen and their be-gowned, bejeweled wives. To a person, the group managed to avert their eyes from this reminder of mortality passing by. When they reached the freight car elevator, the operator's reaction was much the same.

When the doors of a secluded service entrance slammed shut after them, the three men and the gurney stood in the night-shrouded parking lot.

Dr. Hoffman's ambulance was a conveyance of antique vintage. A white paint job did little to improve its appearance. Hoffman stood holding open the rear door so Dave and Devlin could load the gurney into the ambulance. Then Dave slid behind the steering wheel. Hoffman took the passenger seat beside him.

Devlin leaned in to address them through his open side window. He indicated an adjacent row of parked vehicles.

"I'm one lane over. Watch for my lights. Tail me. No siren. I'm going to find us a nice dark alley."

Dave said, "Sounds interesting."

The ambulance stayed behind Devlin's Ford through the heavy nighttime traffic. It was slow going for a few blocks until Devlin found what he was looking for. He angled the Ford into the gloom of an alley that cut between two towering skyscrapers, most of their windows dark for the night. The ambulance turned in behind the Ford. Both vehicles doused their headlights.

Devlin stepped from his car. Background sounds of the

city were vague echoes off building walls, the alley a man-made canyon sealed off from the rest of the world. Hoffman made quick work of unbuckling the gurney's restraints. He stood aside, again serving as doorman. Dave and Devlin transferred Trigger's body from the ambulance to Devlin's car, stretching out the corpse upon the rear seat.

When that task was completed, Dave removed his visored cap and medical whites, beneath which he wore normal street clothing. He tossed the whites onto the passenger seat of the ambulance while Hoffman positioned himself behind the steering wheel.

Devlin said, "Thanks, Doc. Your fee will come through tomorrow."

"Which is why I hope nothing untoward happens to you two this evening," said Hoffman. "Do try to stay alive long enough to pay me. That said, this never happened. Good night, gentlemen."

The ambulance started forward, lights off, Hoffman apparently intending to exit the alley at its opposite end. A front fender of the ambulance loudly banged over a row of garbage cans the doc hadn't seen. He braked and backed up, stopping less than a six inches from bumping into Devlin's car.

"Lights," called Devlin.

A string of curses from Hoffman. Then the headlights came on and the ambulance slowly withdrew without further incident.

"Now what?" asked Dave.

CHAPTER TWENTY-NINE

THEY RETURNED TO THE FORD. Devlin took the wheel.

He said, "How bad do you want to take down Vince Coll?"

Dave settled into the passenger seat. He cast a glance at the dead body resting in the back seat.

"Something tells me this ain't going to be by the book."

"Let's give it a name," said Devlin. "Illegal, with a strong element of personal risk."

"I'm listening."

"I've devised a plan."

"A plan."

"Things click the way I want them to, we're setting Mad Dog Coll up for his execution."

"I'm in."

"Great." Devlin turned on the Ford's headlights. He shifted the car into gear. "Let's find us a telephone booth."

They left the alley. Dave had listened and agreed to Devlin's plan by the time they spotted a drugstore on a relatively quiet cross street, a lighted payphone sign above its entrance. Dave waited in the car. Devlin entered the establishment and sealed himself in the one of the phone booths. Referring to the piece of paper on which he'd jotted the number, he inserted a nickel into the pay phone and dialed.

A male voice answered.

"Yeah?"

Devlin made his voice nervous and reedy.

"Mr. Luciano please."

"Who's calling and why?"

"It's important. I gotta talk to him. It's real important."

"Do better than that. Mr. Luciano's a busy man."

"You don't understand. What I've got will save Lucky's life. I ain't fooling. I gotta talk to him, and I mean right now."

"Hold on."

A thirty-second silence. Devlin wondered if his brilliant plan was being shot down before it even got off the ground. Then a new voice came on. A smooth, cultured voice could not conceal a sharp edge just beneath its surface.

"This better be good. This is a private line. I don't like to be bothered."

"It is good, sir. It's red-hot."

"Who am I talking to?"

"Sir, they call me Trigger."

"State your business. How did you get this number?"

"Sir, I've got something to sell." Devlin pitched his tone higher, rushing the words. "It's about Mr. Coll. It's something you ought to know."

"What about Coll?"

"I heard him talking. He's planning to spring a trap on you, Mr. Luciano. It's all set up."

"What did you say your name was?"

"Wilbur, sir. They call me Trigger."

"Okay, Trigger. Me and you, let's meet. Yeah, we'll do business. I want to know all about this trap. Do you know where I live?"

Devlin knew the address from Luciano's police file.

"Sure, I know it. But we gotta be careful, sir. Coll, he's on to me. I've already ditched one tail tonight. He's setting me up for the kill, I know if he found out I was paying you a call—"

"You're trying my patience, punk."

Devlin paused as if trying to come up with an idea.

Perfect, thought Devlin. His impersonation of dead guy he'd never spoken to was paying off. The crime czar of New York thought he was a nervous, low-level goon, likely flying high on something, fearing for his life because he was ratting out his boss. Just right.

Devlin said, "Can we meet up somewhere dark and quiet? I could tell you what I've got and—"

"Screw that," said Luciano. "You're coming to me, trigger boy. Make tracks over here right now. You got that? I'll be waiting out front with some boys."

"Yes sir, Mr. Luciano. I'm on my way."

Luciano had already broken the connection.

Devlin left the phone booth and returned to the Ford. Except for passing taxicabs and a delivery truck, the quiet block of this off street belonged to the night and to Devlin and Dave. With the dropping temperature of a winter night, few pedestrians were about, mostly bundled-up loners, single-mindedly hurrying to get somewhere. Devlin opened his driver side door and leaned in, reaching across for the glove box.

Dave asked, "How'd it go?"

"Mr. Luciano is waiting on us."

Devlin removed a screwdriver from the glove box. When he returned he was holding the Ford's license plate which he slid under his seat.

Dave said, "Driving without license plates. Won't that get us in trouble with...oh yeah, we are the cops. I keep forgetting."

"It's a one in a million chance that some nosy patrol car pulls us over. But with what we're up to, no license plate numbers to write down and report, well, that's worth the risk."

"And if we are pulled over?"

"We pull rank. We're plainclothes. But that won't happen. and, buddy, we're just getting started. Removing our license plate is the least of it. So are you up for taking the wheel?"

"Said I was in." Dave vacated the passenger seat, walking around the rear of the vehicle to avoid passing before its headlights. He settled behind the steering wheel. "Where to?"

"Lucky and a pack of his gunnies are waiting for us in front of his place, waiting to meet Trigger. We're going to drop Trigger off."

"You've got some imagination, skipper."

"That's what the commish said. He told me to put it to work."

"Should have an interesting result if we get out alive. Hell, even if we don't."

"One more detail," said Devlin.

He climbed into the rear seat. Trigger's corpse was only partially visible, bathed in silver from the lights of the street. Closing the car door after him, Devlin reached under the car seat. He withdrew a toolbox containing various items acquired here and there—maps, a compass, binoculars, and a switchblade knife taken a month ago from a suspect. He returned the box under the seat and opened the knife's 9-inch blade.

He took a deep breath. Then he began plunging the knife blade into the region of the dead man's heart, withdrawing the blade to plunge it again and again with all his strength. The violent sound of the assault filled the confines of the Ford. Devlin stopped at last but only with effort, leaving the blade buried to its hilt in the cadaver's heart. He was surprised to find himself sweating in the cold night air. He was out of breath. Drained.

Dave had turned around to observe. He made a low whistling noise.

"Damn. Never seen anyone stab a dead guy before."

"Has to look good when we drop him off. All the punk left behind when he died was this slab of dead meat in the suit. And we're putting it to good use."

"They might not buy it, Tom. There's no fresh blood. Far as I know, dead guys don't bleed."

"They'll see what we want them to see. They'll buy it because they want to buy it. Ready?"

"Born ready," said Dave. "Let's go."

He shifted the Ford into gear.

CHAPTER THIRTY

WHEN VINCE REGAINED consciousness on the floor of the apartment, he felt like hell. He'd blacked out after Lottie's vicious kick to his nuts. Coming to, it took a few moments for him to recall how he got there.

The sequence of events leading up to that below the belt kick came back to him in a rush—the shootout when those punks came at him in the speakeasy. Hustling the hillbilly singer, Sara Carter. Yeah. Coming home feeling high and fine after that dustup only to find his woman waiting for him with murder on her mind. She knew about the hillbilly broad, and she came at him with the sort of blind rage that only blazed this hot and crazy when the bitch was having her goddamn period.

Vince drew himself to his feet. He massaged his jaw. The intense pain around his groin had faded but his balls would probably ache for a week. Where the hell had she gone? He shook his head, hoping to clear it, supporting himself by leaning against the wall until his vision cleared.

Lottie had likely gone uptown to Harlem. She knew where to score anything she wanted from smoke to nose candy to horse. She used heavy when the monthly curse came upon her. That's it. She'd come home with something to cool her off.

The pressures of their relationship had been building lately. Were they nearing the breaking point? When they first hooked up things had gone well. Even Lottie's recent idea to kidnap other hoods for ransom had turned a handsome profit. Maybe he shouldn't have done what he did to that mug Fratelli, but sometimes it just felt good, as with Fritz, the doorman who fingered him for those punks in the speak. On top of all that was his trouble with Lucky, Dutch, and their mob.

Pressure? Hell, yeah. All of a sudden the whole world seemed to be closing in. Maybe the time had come to end the relationship with Lottie. He could relocate to another city. Philly, maybe...

He made his way across the flat. He kneeled backward on the divan, allowing him to stretch an arm down behind it. He withdrew the bottle he kept hidden there, half full of fine Canadian whiskey from a recent hijack. Lottie wasn't much for housecleaning so he never had to worry about her finding his special bottle. A drink on the rocks, relaxing in his favorite armchair, was just what he needed. They'd straighten things out when she got home.

He crossed to the kitchenette. He poured himself three fingers, opened the icebox for a small block and then reached into the drawer where the icepick was kept. The icepick wasn't there. He stretched his hand deeper into the drawer, feeling around the utensils stored there. And with the jolt of a lightning bolt, everything in his mind cleared. The final recollection fell into place.

Lottie had taken the icepick with her! She'd snagged it from the drawer before the kick, before slamming the door behind her on her way out.

Aw, hell.

Lottie in a fit of jealous rage had taken the icepick with

her. And Vince knew why. Lottie knew about Sara, thanks to Vince and his big mouth. She knew Sara's group was performing tonight at Carnegie Hall. Damn straight things were closing in! Lottie was on her way to murder Sara Carter!

For the briefest moment he considered letting her do it. The crazy broad deserved whatever came her way after something like that, and he sure as hell didn't owe Sara Carter one damn thing. She'd been an interesting piece of hillbilly tail to kid around with but nothing more. He dismissed the thought. With the mob and the cops alike hot to take him down, a crazy, out-of-her-mind homicidal act like that at a time like this could bring everything down on him.

He threw back the shot of whiskey straight. He grabbed his coat off its peg and rushed out into the night. He had to find Lottie.

He had to stop her.

———

THE RAUCOUS NOISE, lights, and excitement of the theater district at show time did not distract Lottie from her mission. A cacophony of beeping horns. Crowded sidewalks. Taxicabs sweeping in to disgorge well-heeled passengers, taking on fresh fares, and zooming away. Distract her? It stoked the emotional fires raging through her. It was all a tunnel of noise with only a single burning light at its end. Her one goal—kill the Carter bitch.

Photographs of the Carter Family and of another performer named Jimmie Rodgers lined either side of Carnegie Hall's front entrance. Lottie paused to study a set of studio photos highlighting each member of the Carter Family. She memorized Sara Carter's features. Plain enough, posed all prim and proper with an autoharp in her lap. Haughty. Regal. A damn cold fish! What the hell did Vince see in something like that? Not that it mattered. Angry as she was at the louse for cheating on her, that's how much venom she felt toward this show business slut he was cheating with. Thought she could steal Lottie Kreisberger's man, did she? The bitch was about to find out differently. Oh, was she ever!

Lottie worked her way around to the rear of the hall where she found less lighting, fewer people, less activity.

She wondered what the hell happened to Trigger. Too chickenhearted to go through with the job she'd sent him on? He was supposed to track and do in this Sara Carter, but she hadn't heard from the punk since sending him on the job. Was Trigger afraid Vince would find out? Either way it was proof that if you wanted something done right, you'd damn well better do it yourself.

The more she thought about it, the more she knew she was on the right track. If Vince was cheating, it wasn't with just this one. When word got around about what she was about to do, that would damn sure stop Vince and his whoring around. And if that didn't work? Well then, she'd kill Vince. The only reason he was big noise was because of the ideas and plans she put in his head. The Fratelli kill that morning showed how over the edge Vince had gone. She could find herself a new man and not miss a beat.

The Carnegie Hall stage door was blocked by a lout who looked like he carried more poundage than intelligence.

"Sorry, miss. Can't let no one in. No autographs, no nothing. Show's already started."

"But it's important," said Lottie with a pout. "You see, I'm with the Carter Family. I have an important message to deliver from back home. Oh, please let me pass."

"Give me the message. I'll see they get it."

"Sure you will." Lottie tried a silky tone, leaning in close, fluttering her eyelashes.

"Isn't there something—*anything*—I could do for you so you'd let me in? I can be very friendly."

The doorman gulped. He looked around.

"Uh, what you got in mind?"

Lottie stepped in, boldly pressing herself against him, her right hand grabbing the front of his trousers. She squeezed and stroked what she found there. She gave him no chance to respond. Ninety seconds later, the lout was bent over, turning away, his eyes embarrassed and hating her.

"Don't say I let you in, you tramp. You got past while my back was turned."

Inside, it was cavernous.

Music and applause carried from beyond the labyrinth of corridors and dressing rooms in which Lottie found herself. She reached into her purse. Her fingers wrapped around the handle of the icepick. Now all she had to do was locate the right dressing room.

And wait...

CHAPTER THIRTY-ONE

JIMMIE RODGERS WAS FLYING HIGH. Sailing. Flat tearing it up. He'd sauntered into the spotlight with that natural nonchalance he never lost. Though he generally preferred sitting on a stool while performing, for this crowd Jimmie stood straight up. Strumming his guitar. Singing his songs.

He opened with "In the Jailhouse Now," giving 'em a taste of his good-natured rounder style, a weary, worldly rambler sharing his dreams and regrets, pleasures and sorrows. This was hardly the sort of audience he was used to, usually performing as he did in honky-tonks and barn dances where folks went early on to hootin' and hollerin' during a performance. Not so here in ol' New York. This audience tonight was dressed to the nines. They sat and listened attentively to each song, taking in the lyrics, followed by polite applause that warmed the hall. Then a hushed silence, ready for the next song.

He played several upbeat numbers after "Jailhouse," songs like "The Mule Skinner Blues," before shifting mid-set to a handful of his more thoughtful, sensitive numbers like "Miss the Mississippi and You" and "Waiting on a Train."

His prolonged standing eventually began wearing on him, the TB pains chiseling away at his stamina.

Damn if he'd let that show at a time like this. He was glad to be singing in the pure indoor air of this great concert hall, nothing like the smoke-hazed juke joints and barn dances where the smoke irritated his lungs and could bring on a coughing fit. This was no damn time for him to hemorrhage! He persevered with the perennial crowd pleaser, "Frankie and Johnnie," then a few romantic tunes. From the rear of the house a few gents even let loose with tentative, half-baked *yee-haws* when they heard "My Rough and Rowdy Ways." Mr. Peer was right. All kinds of folks could enjoy this here music. It occurred to him that this audience of big city folks was in the palm of his hand.

The Carter Family stood in the wings with Mr. Peer. AP, standing next to Peer, was scrutinizing Jimmie's every move, taking in every lyric, observing every audience reaction. Missing nothing. Maybelle held her guitar. Sara held her autoharp in her lap.

There was something different about Sara tonight. Surely understandable after what she'd been through on this day and the pressure she was under tonight. What surprised Jimmie was the fact that Sara did not appear winded or pale after such a day. Quite the opposite. She sat with her back straight, composed and self-possessed. The stoic set of her features and manner possessed a vibrant, healthy glow.

Once onstage, it was impossible to see beyond the stage lights. But before he left the wings, Jimmie had spotted Walter Winchell sitting third row center. Sure enough, the word would certainly be getting out to the world about what was happening here tonight. This audience deserved Jimmie's best, and that's what he was giving them. He might not be long for this world, the damn TB and all, but these folks knew nothing about that. They were getting Jimmie Rodgers in his prime.

He concentrated on keeping his guitar picking simple and clean. He was no great shakes as a guitar player. He knew that. But he also knew how to get the maximum effect out of what he did know, perfectly suiting his playing to each song's lyrics. His voice did not fail him as it sometimes had recently in performances. He was hitting all the right notes, and when he yodeled, his voice glided effortlessly as it always had. He'd be real glad when tonight was done, right satisfied to shake off this big old city.

When he first hit New York this time he'd kept his concerns about the concert—was he up to it, would they like him—under wraps. His characteristic bravado always saw him through. But the whole business of that gunman, Trigger, of tackling someone with a knife hell-bent on murder, and then holding a gun on the young fellow before locking him away so the kid could drink himself to death on bad whiskey that had been meant for Jimmie...it all combined to sour him. Guns. Knives. Bad whiskey. Dead bodies. He'd had his fill of New York.

He concluded his set with the one that always proved to be a crowd favorite, "Carolina Sunshine Girl," leaving them with that rounder attitude seasoned with romance and a smile. How could you top a combination like that? The folks in New York seemed to agree. Their applause nearly blew the roof off.

DUTCH AND LUCKY stood in the vestibule of the high-rise. Beyond plate glass that bordered a modest front entrance, Park Avenue was a noisy, vibrating night scene, an endless flow of buses, trucks, taxis, and pedestrians. A cold night, a stiff breeze cutting through the city streets.

The vestibule was not warm or comfortable. The floor, cold marble. An elevator faced the entrance. A night watchman/doorman, usually seated at a small desk off to the side, had sensed trouble brewing and was nowhere in sight. Four gunmen, posted outside the front entrance, made no effort to meld with the passing pedestrians. Tight-lipped and grim in their winter coats, Lucky's men eyed carefully every approaching vehicle and person.

Dutch observed, imagining a vehicle racing by. A machine gunner or two leaning out its windows riddling the vestibule and the men in it with gunfire.

He said, "You think maybe we're being set up? Coll is just crazy enough to try something like that."

"Let him," said Lucky. He fired up a cigarette. "It cost me a bundle when I moved into this dump, but I had them install bulletproof glass. And my boys have their eyes peeled." The hint of a small smile. "Don't worry, Dutch. You're safe when you're standing next to me."

Dutch thought, you prick.

He said, "I just get edgy waiting for something to happen. So now you know where the punk and his moll are hid out. I've got me a hit team with a tommy-gun standing by. They'll drop the hammer on that boy. I can make it happen with one phone call."

"I know that. But Dutch, we're talking a new game, remember? It's all set. The other bosses on the board will approve the hit *if* Coll steps out of line one more time."

"Even after that massacre at the speak? He killed three guys in full view of witnesses."

"Yes, but he was defending himself. That gets him a pass. I don't like it, but if we want this to work, there it is. We've got to keep this new alliance perfectly lined up with the other bosses. Right now trust is at a minimum. I want to clinch the new setup. It's a trial case. One more unsanctioned hit by Coll, and you make your call."

"You want my opinion, Lucky, we shoulda rubbed out that mad dog this morning after what he did to Arn Fratelli."

"It's a new world, Dutch. Besides, I want to hear what this punk Trigger has to tell me about our friend Vince."

The high revving of a car's engine cut through the street noise outside. The gun crew were in the process of pawing for concealed hardware when the Ford coupe came speeding by. Its rapid acceleration caused pedestrians to leap aside for safety. Other vehicles braked to avoid a collision. The Ford went flying by so fast, when a human body was ejected from it, the body went into a somersault before rolling twice and coming to a stop in the gutter directly in front of the high-rise. By the time the gunmen had their pistols in hand, the Ford was already a half-block away. It went round the next corner on two squealing wheels, disappearing from sight.

Lucky hurried out onto the sidewalk, Dutch right behind him. Lucky waved down his men.

"Stow the heat."

Dutch went to the body, rolling the corpse over onto its back. A knife handle protruded prominently from its chest. Dutch patted the body down, finding a wallet. He extracted a driver's license.

Lucky called over, "Well?"

"Says here his name is Wilbur W. Feldstein."

"That's him. Wilbur. Called himself Trigger. That's the punk was coming to see me."

"Looks like Vince Coll got to him first." Dutch lifted a sheaf of bills from the wallet. He folded and pocketed the money before tossing the wallet onto the corpse. He rejoined Lucky. "Our boy Vinnie's been a busy little son of a bitch today, hasn't he?"

Lucky motioned his men toward the body.

"Get that damn thing out of here. Take it around to that alley over there. I don't care what you do with it but make sure the stiff disappears. Got me?"

"Yes, sir," replied the crew boss.

The exchange was so low, with all of the surrounding

street noises Dutch could barely overhear. Around them, passersby used to minding their own business began slowing for a look, sensing something unusual happening here, starting to show interest. The crew of thugs hauled the body up out of the gutter and carried it away. This being New York, no one objected or tried to interfere.

Within a minute after the crew entered the alley with the body, the flow of pedestrians and vehicular traffic passing the high-rise had resumed as if nothing had happened.

Dutch said, "Now what?"

Lucky flipped his cigarette into the gutter.

"Make that call."

CHAPTER THIRTY-TWO

MAYBELLE'S HEART soared with joy.

They were sounding great! Her fingers weren't missing a chord or a lick on the guitar. With her sparse, effective playing, Sara's autoharp, and AP providing accompaniment on guitar and with vocal harmonies, Sara's voice was soaring over the audience.

They'd begun with "My Clinch Mountain Home," a musical calling card intended to introduce them. Except for AP's railroad song, "Wabash Cannonball," Sara did all the singing, her glorious voice conveying stories in songs of love, regret, hope, and hard times. Sara was delivering flawless vocal renditions of a wide range of their repertoire from a heartfelt "Wildwood Flower" to the one that always got a knowing reaction from the womenfolk, "Single Girl, Married Girl," about a young mother rocking her baby while she recalls her carefree life before marriage.

Mr. Peer never budged from his observation post in the wings, hands clasped behind his back, rocking back and forth in time to the music. Listening closely, he nodded with approval as the set progressed. As with Jimmie Rodgers, the

Yankees seemed to be respectful of this brand of music. They sat there and listened, offering up polite applause after each selection. Almost like a secular church, if that made sense. This audience was in the palm of her hand!

How far their lives had come since that first audition for Mr. Peer in Bristol. She could see and feel it all as if it happened only yesterday. Upstairs in a gloomy warehouse loft. Walls hung with blankets. A recording machine. The strange cylindrical microphone on a stand. Mr. Peer with his new wife and two engineers to operate the recording machine. Mrs. Peer was a sophisticate, every bit as businesslike as her husband. She ushered the children into a corner, distracting them with ice cream while the Carter Family mounted the little wooden stage, drew close to one another and sang into a microphone for the first time, Maybelle's guitar leading the way, Sara and AP coming in right on cue. From there began the journey to this performance in the stage lights of Carnegie Hall.

Maybelle's mind seldom wandered during performance. But on this night as she strummed and watched and listened to Sara mesmerize an audience, Maybelle found herself wondering and worrying.

What a day this had been.

Of the two of them, Sara had always been the serious one. Maybelle was proud of her guitar playing, but Sara was the one who always seemed to know how to dress, what to say, how to stand in front of a microphone and sing her heart out no matter how she felt. Serious. Always serious. She took her singing seriously because she understood how her voice had the power to move people. She always gave a good performance. Maybelle only wished Sara could love and enjoy performing as much as Maybelle and AP did. She never seemed enthused about working on the road. Sara would rather be sitting on the porch, playing for friends.

This hadn't become a problem...yet. Perhaps it never would. But it was always there, an undercurrent that Maybelle sensed deepening the romantic entanglements of the preceding summer.

Tonight Sara's performance was flawless. The applause grew more enthusiastic and went on longer with each number. AP's countenance as he played his guitar and harmonized along, while not quite glowing, at least became less dour than usual as the set went on. That's how good they were sounding! Sara appeared lost in the music, her carried away as always. There was no hint of the battered emotions Sara displayed earlier in their hotel room. Quite the opposite. Mrs. Carter appeared to be infused with a new, stronger energy than ever before, as if she was building up a head of steam while performing.

Sara looked ready to take on the world.

———

DEVLIN GLIDED his Ford to the curb. The tree-lined residential street, a quiet working-class neighborhood, was mostly dark at this hour. A single lighted window shone from the duplex where Dave Heyer lived with his wife and their baby girl.

The Ford's license plate was properly re-affixed. Dave again rode in the front passenger seat, appearing normal enough after having shoved a corpse from a speeding car minutes earlier. He sent Devlin a grin.

"Gotta say, skipper, thanks for an interesting evening."

"Thank you," said Devlin. "Tonight gets filed under above and beyond the call of duty. To quote Dr. Hoffman, this never happened. The fewer people know about our stunt, the better."

"Glad to hear it before they start calling us the Gangster

Squad because we act like gangsters. We'd be back to pounding a beat or worse. What about Lucky and Dutch. Think they bought it?"

"They did if we did our job, and I think we did."

"What about the commissioner? Is he going to hear about this?"

"I don't think the commissioner wants to hear about it. All he wants is Coll dead."

"Well, mission accomplished on that score. G'night, skipper."

Dave cast his gaze in the direction of that lighted window in the duplex where the silhouette of a woman holding a baby was clearly discernible.

Devlin said, "You really love them, don't you, Dave?"

"What do you think? Marla's the best. I'd take a bullet for either one of those two."

"Know what I'd do if I were you?"

"Tell me."

"I'd quit the force. I'd leave New York. Yesterday would be soon enough. Find yourself a little burg out in the country somewhere where you and your little family can live the rest of your lives happily ever after."

Dave said, "Huh. Well, I'll always take your advice to heart, skipper. But that sure as hell sounds extreme if you don't mind me saying so, especially after tonight. Don't you worry about Dave Heyer on account of I'm a standup guy who can take care of himself. I'll protect what's mine."

"I know that, Dave. I don't want to spoil the party. But when you're holding those two in your arms, and you want that feeling to last forever, think about what I said. Okay?"

"Damn. You talk like poet. No offense."

"None taken. Call it advice from experience. I'll try not to bring it up again. Night, Dave."

Dave stepped from the Ford.

"You done for the night?"

"I will be after one more stop," said Devlin. "I want to catch up with those folks at Carnegie Hall. Give them a report. Up to a point, that is. It'll be nice to socialize with some respectable citizens for a change."

CHAPTER THIRTY-THREE

SARA DABBED AWAY the last of what they called "greasepaint" from her face. Supposedly the ointment had made her more visible in the stage lights to even those in the far back seats. Another aspect of "show business" that came as part and parcel of this much ballyhooed performance.

It was over. The concert, the ordeal, was over.

Thank God.

The dressing room was a simple affair dominated by a vanity table with an oversized, three-panel, hinged makeup mirror before which she now sat. A single window, closed against the winter. Room enough to accommodate a trunk or two. A closet large enough to accommodate costume changes, props and so forth, empty now. She had arrived this evening with only her purse and her beloved autoharp. The instrument, secure in its case, now rested in a corner next to the vanity.

One could hardly *not* luxuriate in the personal privacy that came with having one's own dressing room. This was a first. Most places the Carter Family played down home didn't have dressing rooms. Heck, some of them didn't even have restrooms! She chuckled at the thought.

The concert had gone off without a hitch. Folks generally seemed to like the group. She would never be comfortable with gushing praise. It was enough to know that an audience enjoyed, perhaps took heart in, the stories she sang for them. Their brand of "mountain music" (as the concert program labeled it) had gone over in a big way. Mr. Peer was highly pleased. Even AP's dour countenance had warmed. AP had wanted to speak with her after they got off stage. Sara managed to excuse herself soon as she could without appearing rude to the others. And so here she sat applying a light touch of makeup from her purse.

She was proud of her reflection in the mirror. She looked her age, yes. But men still found her attractive. She knew enough about men to read that much in their eyes. And yet her reflection in this mirror tonight looked...different. How had she changed? She could see the answer to that one in her eyes. Or maybe, she thought, I *am* different after this day and this night.

There had never been such a day. A life-changing concert, that is, if it led to the fame and riches Mr. Peer was predicting, and a life-changing, traumatic explosion of unleashed violence when she stole away to meet Vince. A hoodlum sent to kill her in a high-tone hotel. Life changing? Life *ending* for the poor souls murdered before her eyes in that speakeasy. Life was so fragile. It could be snatched from you without warning in the blink of an eye. Amid everything else from that horror emerged one truth. One had durn well better live life for oneself before that final moment came. This did not mean dodging commitments or being free as a bird. She had children to raise. She wanted to be a good mother to her kids.

She was concentrating on applying eye liner when someone opened the door behind her and entered the dressing room. Must be Maybelle, she told herself, come for an after-show visit. Then she heard the door lock click. That wouldn't be Maybelle. The day had brought an edge to her awareness. She set down the eye liner brush. Whoever it was angled aside to avoid casting a reflection in the mirror. She started to turn, started to speak, not alarmed but curious about who was letting themself in uninvited. She thought, it better not be AP.

Turning on the stool is what saved her life.

A woman she'd never seen before—well-dressed, a slim brunette who might've been pretty but for the insane rage twisting features—came charging at her, an icepick in her raised hand! Bringing the icepick down with killing force! Hissing like an animal!

If Sara hadn't turned upon hearing the click of the lock, the blade of the icepick would have sunk into her back. It missed her by fractions of an inch. The assailant's arm impacted Sara's shoulder, knocking both women off balance. Sara stumbled a few steps from the stool before regaining her footing, her back pressed against the wall. The woman regained her balance. Her eyes glared wide with madness. The icepick raised again, about to strike.

The woman snarled, "Nice try, bitch. But only one of us is leaving this room alive. You lay with my man, you die!"

She lunged at Sara. Sara bent her knees slightly, grasping the stool with both hands, swinging it around to hold up before her defensively as a shield.

"Stop! Who are you? What are you doing? What's this about?"

Her assailant, temporarily held at bay, paused long enough to spew, "What's it about? It's about you thinking you can steal Vince Coll. I kill trespassers. Who am I? I'm your executioner!"

Their eyes locked across the held-up stool like duelists locking eyes over crossed swords. Having recovered from her initial surprise, Sara found herself clearheaded.

"But that's crazy! I don't want your man. I've got a

husband. I'm a singer from Tennessee. I'm going home tomorrow."

"Yeah, you're going home. You're going home in a pine box!" There came a knock at the door. Someone tried the knob. They'd been drawn by this commotion.

Maybelle's voice: "Sara, what's going on in there? Are you okay?"

Mr. Peer: "Mrs. Carter, let us in. Is everything all right?"

Sara maintained eye contact with the woman. She spoke to those at the door.

"Everything's fine. I'll be right there." Then she said to the intruder, trying to sound rational addressing those wildly raging eyes, "I might be wearing makeup and a dress, but dang your hide, whoever you are, I'm a country woman. Think you're tough, do you? You wouldn't last a day on the farm. And by the way, I was raised with three brothers. It's been a while, but they taught me how to fight."

With every ounce of strength she could muster, Sara used the stool held between them to forcefully shove the woman against the opposite wall. Then she jerked her grip on the stool. A leg of the stool smashed her opponent's wrist against the edge of the makeup table. No good. The woman retained her grip of the icepick and came at Sara again.

Sara flung the stool aside, planted her feet firmly the way she'd been taught. Her left arm came up to parry the thrust coming at her. Her right fist balled, and she delivered a sharp right punch to the intruder's jaw that stopped the woman in her tracks, her eyes rolling back in their sockets. With a weary sigh she collapsed like a puppet with its strings cut. Her eyes were closed, and she did not move.

The knocking at the door had become more fervent, as did the inquiring voices.

Sara stood silent for a moment. She took a deep breath. Exhaled. Her right hand was rock steady, the knuckles skinned. She blew on them to cool their prickly sting, her senses sharp and clear as if having been injected with some sort of pick-me-up. She opened the door.

Maybelle and Mr. Peer greeted her appearance with expressions of concern that dissolved into relief. AP and Jimmie Rodgers could be seen hurrying in along with a handful of members of the backstage crew.

Maybelle said, "Good gracious, Sara, it sounded like a riot going on in there!"

She was trying with undisguised curiosity to peer around Sara's shoulder, into the interior of the dressing room. Beside her, Mr. Peer likewise stood angling for a look.

"Mrs. Carter, should I call the law?"

A new voice said, "The law's already here. What's the trouble?"

Detective Devlin approached, joining them from Sara's blind side, from the direction of the backstage door.

Sara had drawn the dressing room door shut behind her. After all, Mr. Peer was the boss. He would know how to handle this. She would wait a minute or so for this little flurry of excitement to blow over, for this gathering of people to disperse. Then she would let Mr. Peer into the dressing room to deal with the unconscious woman.

Mr. Peer said, "So good to see you, Detective. We're trying to determine if there's been any trouble. " He sent Sara a meaningful glance.

There was a windblown look about Devlin, but his presence, the arrival of the law, changed everything.

"There's trouble aplenty," she told them. "I've just been attacked a second time today."

Mr. Peer blinked. "Good Lord!"

Maybelle said, "So that's what we heard! What happened?"

"A woman came at me with an icepick. I, uh, had to knock her out."

Those within earshot dropped their jaws.

Devlin said, "Let's take a look."

Stepping past Sara, he opened the door. Sara followed him in. The others gathered behind her in the doorway.

The dressing room was empty. The window yawned wide open. Its draperies flapped, dancing in the frigid air rushing in.

Sara's heart sank.

"But I left her less than a minute ago!"

"She was either faking," said Maybelle, "or she made one fast recovery."

Mr. Peer said, "She can't have gone far."

"I'll catch her before she does," said Devlin.

He hoisted himself through the open window without effort and disappeared into the night.

CHAPTER THIRTY-FOUR

DROPPING TO THE PAVEMENT, Devlin crouched in a walkway that ran past the window, a pocket of gloom apart from where the night shimmered with bright lights, noise, people and traffic. The wind whistling down the narrow areaway whipped at the tails of Devlin's coat. A pang of disappointment surged through him. No sign of anyone back here. Was he too late? Had Sara Carter's assailant made her escape?

At the far end of the walkway a taxicab braked to a stop. A man and a woman hurriedly boarded, a tall man holding open the door, gesturing for the woman to hurry. Even from a distance, Vince Coll was recognizable in the street lights. That made the woman Lottie Kreisberger. The woman with the ice pick! The assailant. And they were making their getaway.

Had Coll sent her? Was he behind her attack on Mrs. Carter? No time to puzzle that out now. Reaching for his pistol, Devlin started in the direction of the taxi. Coll sensed movement coming at him from the walkway. Without hesitation he drew a pistol and fired twice in that direction, the twin reports loud enough to reverberate through the city noise.

Devlin flung himself to the pavement. The bullets whistled over his head. Then came the slam of a car door and the cab was gone. Devlin holstered his pistol. He hurried from the mouth of the walkway, finding a line of cabs idling at the curb, waiting for fares that hadn't yet straggled from the concert. Folks were staring after receding lights of the departed taxi.

Devlin ran to the first taxi in the line. The cabbie was a wiry, freckle-faced fellow in his thirties, chawing a toothpick and listening to a football game on his car radio.

Devlin said, "That cab that just tore out. Can you tail it without tipping them off?"

"I'm a New York cab driver, bub. I can do anything."

Devlin flung himself into the cab.

"Then get on it."

———

VINCE TWISTED AROUND, peering out through the rear window of his taxi, searching for any indication that they were being followed. Impossible to tell due to the heavy traffic dominated by taxicabs.

He said to the driver, "Can you tell if we're being tailed?"

"I...I can't tell, sir. I don't think so."

The driver was a nervous punk no more than 20, green as hell and jittery after Vince fired those rounds to discourage anyone interested enough to give chase.

What the hell had Lottie done back there, in Carnegie Hall of all places, to cause such a stir? Must have had something to do with that hillbilly singer he'd dallied with. Screw it. He settled back in his seat, regarding Lottie who sat beside him, stiff-backed. Staring straight ahead. Fists clenched. Her mouth was a taut, angry gash in a pale, drawn face. She reminded Vince of a statue carved in ice.

He said, "You going to tell me what happened?"

Lottie said nothing.

She hadn't said a word since he'd found her climbing out of that window. He'd been reconnoitering, trying to decide what to do next, when he caught her making her escape. Escape from what? He didn't know. The hell with it, he decided. And the hell with Lottie. This crazy business was the last straw. It was time to move on. In the beginning she'd given him a lot of good ideas, and the hot stuff Lottie dished out in bed made up for always having to deal with the shrew she became when things didn't go her way. Who knows what would've happened if the cops had taken her into custody. It was time to cover his tracks and move on, yeah.

Everything was changing. Within a year the repeal of prohibition would become a reality. Lucky Luciano and his "syndicate" were already moving into other rackets, becoming more organized by the day. It was no longer feasible to continue with Lottie's idea of kidnapping other mobsters for ransom. Arn Fratelli would be the last. A new racket was needed.

The nearer their cab got to the Cornish Arms, the clearer these simple facts became in his mind. Hell, he needed a new everything! A new racket. A new woman. And it came to him like a bolt out of the blue—he needed a new *city*. A new area of operations where he could set up shop. That's it! New York had become too damn hot for him.

He would catch a train and ride. They said Philadelphia was a place where a guy with ambition could make something of himself. That's what he'd do. Set up shop in Philly. Send for his best boys like Trigger. Where the hell was Trigger anyway? But that's what he'd do. Sounded better that dodging bullets and the law on a daily basis in New York.

Lottie didn't want to talk? Fine, there would be no good-byes. He would phone Grand Central. Find out when the next redeye was leaving for Philly. And he'd be on it wearing the clothes on his back and the gun under his arm. Time for a new start, hell yeah. He wouldn't even go back tonight to their apartment. Lottie would only find some way to mess with him. There was a line of telephone booths in the pharmacy across the street from the Cornish Arms. When they got to the hotel, he'd walk across the street call to make a reservation on the next thing smoking. He'd never see Lottie again.

His new life would begin.

———

DEVLIN'S DRIVER knew his stuff.

He paced Coll's taxi, trailing steadily at a half-dozen car lengths. It couldn't have been easy through the heavy traffic. The uptown theaters—plays and movies—were all letting out with the restaurants and cabarets in full swing. A few times Devlin lost track of which among the many taxicabs they were supposed to be following. His driver, intent at the steering wheel, never losing track.

Devlin leaned back in his seat. Nothing to do now but wait to see where he was being led. He felt strangely relaxed. The enraged slamming of that knife into a dead man's chest had somehow purged him of the intense rage that had been driving him. He still had that anger deep down, but he was seeing things more clearly. This was about the future. Ralph Peer and his bunch wanted to start a record industry, put the songs of America into the ears of every American who wanted to listen. Lucky and Dutch wanted to create a national crime syndicate that would have its extorting hand in every form of legal business. If there was ever a time to boost one and quash the other, now was that time.

He would arrest Lottie. And Coll? This would be their second confrontation of the day. Despite the stunt he and Dave had just staged to put Coll in the mob's crosshairs, there was no reason to dodge the personal confrontation that was the surely about to occur. Matter of fact, this sounded like the perfect way to end this day. Devlin glanced at his wrist watch in the passing street lights. A minute past midnight. Call it the start of a new day. He drew his .38 from its shoulder holster, checking the weapon's load and action. If the driver heard the clicking gun sounds, he didn't let on. His eyes remained glued to those taillights.

Backup would be nice. Anything could happen in the next few minutes. He was a cop again putting his life on the line. And if he survived, then what? As a cop taking on the criminal element terrorizing the city, after tonight he'd damn well feel he'd done his part. Maybe he should take the advice he'd given Dave. He didn't want to lose his family. Had he thrown it all away, or was there still a chance of saving their marriage?

The taxi they were tailing swung off Eighth Avenue onto 23rd, a secondary street of moderate traffic. The cab drew to the curb before a plain, ten-story structure of brown brick. A lighted marquee over the front entrance proclaimed *Cornish Arms Hotel*. Small storefront businesses lined the street, most of them closed at this hour. The only open, well-lighted storefront was *The London Chemists*, a drugstore across the street from the residential hotel.

Devlin's cab sailed past the hotel.

"Good work," said Devlin. "Bring us around."

"Gotcha."

The driver steered them into a smooth U-turn, parking at the curb a half-block away opposite the Cornish Arms, three doors down from the pharmacy. He doused the headlights, letting the engine idle.

Devlin could clearly observe Coll paying off his driver.

Lottie was not waiting on him. When the cab drove off, she had already disappeared into the hotel. Coll did not follow her in. He strode across street to the drugstore.

Devlin said, "Wait here.'"

"Glad to," said the cabbie. "But, uh, something tells me now would be a good time to pay your fare. Uh, just in case."

Devlin chuckled. The driver had heard the gun sounds from the backseat. He paid his fare with a generous tip. Then he considered his options. He could either follow Coll into the pharmacy or wait out on the sidewalk until Coll came out. Lottie could be dealt with later, it being better for now to have her out of the way. And what if the mad dog simply surrendered?

Devlin started out of the cab, hesitating when something up the street caught his attention. A sleek sedan, a Hudson Cruiser parked several car lengths from the Cornish Arms, drew away from that curb without headlights to make a U-turn and stop directly in front of the pharmacy, well ahead of Devlin's cab. Devlin settled back in his seat to see what would happen.

A man toting a Thompson submachine gun emerged from the passenger side of the Hudson Cruiser. The weapon wasn't hard to miss in the lights of the drugstore as he stepped inside.

Devlin's driver said, "What the hell?"

Devlin's gun was still in his hand.

He said, "It's going to get noisy in a minute."

He'd barely spoken when, from the direction of the pharmacy, the loud hammering roar of a submachine gun, firing on full-auto, pierced the night.

The driver said, "Yowza."

The guy with the Thompson emerged from the drugstore at a run. He flung the machine gun into the rear of the sedan and threw himself into the front seat. The Cruiser tore away from the curb with a squeal of tires, its headlights flicking on. Tires squealed again as it ran a red light and sped up 8ᵗʰ Avenue, disappearing from sight.

Devlin said to the driver, "Are you game?"

"Not this time, bub. Those boys play for keeps."

"Wise man."

Devlin left the taxi, holstering his .38 in its concealed shoulder holster. Lottie was still around and would need to be dealt with. But first things first. Pedestrians were always about in New York even at this hour. A small number of them were tentatively gathering around the pharmacy. Devlin made his way inside, knowing what he'd find.

A haze of gun smoke lingered in the air, the floor scattered with brass shell casings. Two male pharmacy clerks and a woman customer were crouched behind counters at the rear of the store. An elderly man sat on a stool at the soda fountain counter. Terror was in their eyes, their mouths agape. A row of three phone booths faced the counter. The booth on the far end had been shot to pieces. Glass and shards of wood were everywhere. The phone inside dangled at the end of its cord, a dial tone faintly audible.

Vince Coll lay face down on the floor, a bloody mess. His long legs were stretched out straight, his feet in the remains of the phone booth. He was dead.

Devlin flashed his badge to those present.

"Relax, everyone. It's over."

"Thank heavens," said the man at the counter. Like everyone else, he could not take his eyes off the corpse. "The fellow with the machine gun...he walked right in. 'Keep cool now,' he told us. Then he opened fire."

At that moment, Lottie Kreisberger emerged from the small crowd blocking the front entrance. One look at the body on the floor, and she emitted a high bleat of sound that could barely be called human. She ran in and fell to her knees beside Vince. She began sobbing hysterically.

"Oh, my Vincent...the dirty rats! Oh, the dirty rats."

Then she was pounding on him angrily with clenched fists, crying out things like, "You dirty cheating bastard! I hate you!" before reverting to sobbing moans. "Oh, darling Vincent, why did you have to die?"

Her wailing was soon joined by the whining wail of approaching sirens.

CHAPTER THIRTY-FIVE

February 8, 1932

SARA HARDLY SLEPT a wink that night.

How could she? New York. Flirtation with a big city gangster. Two—count them, *two!*—assaults on her life. Socking a woman on the jaw in self-defense. And worst of all, the living nightmare of seeing people, everyday human beings, slaughtered in a bloody massacre. Her mind would not, could not stop, keeping her awake. Gradually she sensed the mighty Waldorf-Astoria awakening around her.

In the gray light of a cold dawn, scant conversation passed between her, AP, and Maybelle during a taxicab ride to the station. Jimmie Rodgers was long gone, having chosen not to spend another night in the big town. During the night, he'd caught a redeye to Memphis where he had bookings lined up.

Mr. Peer had arranged a first-class compartment for the Carter Family aboard the train now carrying them home. A token, he'd said, of his appreciation for a job exceedingly well done. Before bidding their little group a fond farewell in the Waldorf lobby, he informed them of last night's outcome concerning the woman, Lottie Kreisberger, and Vincent Coll. And he had strongly recommended that, in the interests of maintaining good publicity and propriety, no mention should ever be made of Sara's involvement with the criminal element, not even to members of their own families. That sounded like a good idea to all involved.

The train trip north had wearied and drained Sara. On this return ride, with every mile the train traveled, she could feel a calm sense of relief and accomplishment returning. Maybelle and AP surely would be feeling that same sense of pride and accomplishment. Their eyes had begun drooping even before the train left the station. Sara sat gazing out the train window at the passing scene. The dense urban neighborhoods began to gradually thin and fall away as the train gained speed.

Her mind wandered to the police detective, Devlin, who showed up on the station platform just as they were boarding. Sara had sort of expected him, though she made no mention of it when he appeared. At least she was not surprised.

The detective was a brave, forthright man. He'd played such a key role in yesterday, it was only natural such a man would check in with them at the windup. Devlin was an observant man, being a detective. He'd spotted Sara's bruised knuckles and grinned a little grin. Sara wondered what else he could see. She saw a restless hurt in his eyes. The sort of hurt she knew all too well.

The first thing he said was, "Thought I'd come by to wish you folks a safe journey home. New York's been pretty rough on you. Hope you won't hold it against us."

Sara said, "Not at all, Detective. Thank you for everything you've done."

Maybelle, with that sweet, diplomatic smile of hers, added, "Reckon we did meet some fine folks up here, and you sure was one of 'em. Ain't that right, AP?"

AP had put in his two cents with of a gruff, "Much obliged for all you done, Devlin."

"Yes indeed," said Sara. "Thank you for trying to warn me in that speakeasy yesterday. You were so right. I'm much obliged to you."

"Glad to be of service," said Devlin. "You folks are leaving New York better than you found it," said Devlin. "Lottie Kreisberger is in a cell, and the city is done with Mad Dog Coll. Sorry I missed your show. I came down to offer you best wishes for a safe trip home."

The train whistle sounded. A conductor called all aboard.

AP added, "Come along then, Sara. You too, Maybelle. Don't want this here train leaving without us."

Sara bristled. It's just how he's used to talking to me, she told herself. I'll break him of it. She caught Devlin's eye. They exchanged a nod. Then she and Maybelle followed AP aboard the train.

And so here she sat, watching the New Jersey scenery roll past the train window. A new day was awakening out there in the world...and in her life. What they said was true. Those hard times that didn't destroy you could make you stronger.

She was Mrs. AP Carter. The wife of a man she did not love. She would continue this career of travel and performance. Times were hard. She would provide for her family. She would do nothing to alter the detached, regal impression with which she carried herself. That was her defense, the invisible wall she'd constructed to protect herself in a world she would never feel comfortable in. Maybelle would be there for comfort and companionship. Sara Carter would honor her commitments. Onstage she would always give her best. But she would never again be swept along through life like aimless driftwood on a river. And she would not die without knowing love. Coy Bays would live forever deep in her heart...

AP's droning voice drew her from reverie. He was reading aloud from a tabloid newspaper. The tabloid headline read KILLER COLL SLAIN.

"Says here after they took him to the morgue, they took a total of fifteen bullets out of that feller Coll's body. Says they figure the same number of slugs likely passed through him. Dang. That's what I call dead."

Was AP trying to needle her? If so, that was another thing she'd have to break him of.

Maybelle said, "It'd suit me just fine if I never see New York again. I reckon folks could be living satisfied in a place like that. But I don't see how."

Sara said, "Amen to that."

AP folded the newspaper, set it aside.

"Every path in life has its own hardships and sacrifices. Further north we go, them city folks take some getting used to. They think we're simple. Call us yokels, hicks, hillbillies. But they got it worse. Everyone acting devious-like. Money-hungry. Neurotic. They see a man down, they don't try to help him none. They give him a kick in the teeth. That ain't no way to live."

Those were the most words Sara could remember hearing from AP in quite some time. She didn't want to engage too much in conversation with the man, but it was important he and Maybelle know, as they were heading home, where her sentiments rested.

Maybelle said, "Life in the city sure 'nuff 'pears to be hard going. The constant noise of traffic day and night. And the air! Filled with dust and soot. Why, it's as if the earth itself is smothered beneath all that concrete, steel, and cement. Country living is the best."

AP nodded.

"The works of humanity cannot compare to the works of nature."

Sara thought, well ain't we a profound bunch!

She said, "It'll be good to wake up down home where morning is when a soul can feel creation, and the world is still quiet, that's for dang sure."

AP resumed reading his newspaper. No longer aloud, thank heavens.

Maybelle unlatched her guitar case. Removing the instrument, she began idly strumming a lilting melody unfamiliar to Sara.

Tonight Sara would say a prayer for Detective Devlin. He noticed her bruised knuckles? Well, she noticed that he wore a wedding ring. And the hurt she saw in his eyes? His private life. He'd stepped into the mess that was yesterday and proceeded to straighten the whole mess out. Only a woman could cause hurt in the eyes of such a man. Did Devlin's wife understand what she had in a man like that? Sara would fight to hold onto a man like Thomas Devlin. Or would she? She did love such a man. His name was Coy Bays. Only that hadn't worked out so well, had it?

Maybelle strummed her guitar, a soothing counterpoint to the constant clickety clack of railroad noise.

AP dozed.

Sara went back to gazing out the train window at a world passing by.

AFTERWORD

The novel you have just read is a combination of truth and fiction.

The musicians, the gangsters, and Mr. Ralph Peer were real people. Tom Devlin is a product of my imagination as are all of the scenes he appears in, as is the entire plot of southern musicians interacting with the New York underworld. That's fiction. The Carter Family's Carnegie Hall concert also never happened, although thirty years later an aggregation of family members did perform there in a concert tribute to the original Carter Family, who became known as the First Family of country music.

Most of the crimes attributed here to Mad Dog Coll are based on fact. Except for Devlin's involvement, Coll's murder occurred much as I've depicted it, including Lottie showing up and throwing herself hysterically across his fresh corpse. Coll was buried next to his brother Peter in the Bronx. Dutch Schultz sent a floral wreath bearing a banner that read *From the Boys*.

Believe it or not, Lottie Kreisberger too was a real person. A newspaper writer of the day labeled her "the quintessential gun moll." She is regarded, then and now, as the power behind Coll. What happened to Lottie? No one seems to know. She's vanished into the mists of time, dropping out of sight not long after Coll's murder. It's generally assumed Lottie met her fate at the hands of those who rubbed out Vince, although rumors persist that she reinvented herself, changed her name, and died a respectable dowager sometime in the 1950s.

Although Sara and AP separated in 1933, the act as I've portrayed them remained a working unit for years. AP eventually left the music business in 1943 to run a general store. He died in Kingsport, Tennessee in 1960. Maybelle went on to become a widely respected matriarchal figure in the country music field. She and her daughters toured through the 1960s, often with Maybelle's son-in-law, Johnny Cash. Maybelle died in 1978.

Jimmie Rodgers, in New York for a recording session, died there on May 26, 1933. Widely regarded as the Father of Country Music, he has been cited as an inspiration by countless country singers. Ralph Peer continued his career as an eminently successful businessman in the music industry until his passing in 1960.

Lucky Luciano's gunmen executed Dutch Schultz in the men's room of a Newark restaurant in 1935. Luciano is considered the architect of modern organized crime. He reigned supreme until his death of a heart attack in Italy in 1962. He'd gone to the airport to meet with an American movie producer about a film based on his life.

The newspaper quote attributed to Walter Winchell in Chapter 25 did in fact appear in his *Daily Mirror* column the day before Vince Coll's murder. Following his career in radio, Winchell's most notable legacy was his breathless narration of the 1960s hit TV show *The Untouchables*. He died in 1972.

And Sara Carter?

By 1939, the Carters were appearing on national radio

every weekday evening. *The Good Neighbor Get-Together* was broadcast live out of Del Rio, Texas. There'd been no communication between Sara and Coy Bays for several years when, one cold February night, Sara stepped up to the microphone and improvised, dedicating a song, "I'm Thinking Tonight of My Blue Eyes," *to Coy Bays in California*. Coy was listening to the radio that night. Upon hearing the show, he promptly drove the 1200 miles to Del Rio where he and Sara Carter were married on March 8, 1939. Sara gave up her performing career (except for occasional appearances over the years with Maybelle) and returned with Coy to California where they spent the rest of their lives together. Sara died in 1979.

ACKNOWLEDGMENTS

My portrayal of these people and the world they lived in is largely based on research from the following sources:

Will You Miss Me When I'm Gone? by Mark Zwonitzer with Charles Hirschberg, a thorough and brilliantly rendered account of the Carter Family.

Mad Dog Coll: An Irish Gangster by Breandan Delap and Rich Gold. All you'll ever need to know about Vincent Coll, Dutch Schultz, Lucky Luciano, and their gang wars.

Jimmie Rodgers: The Life and Times of America's Blue Yodeler by Nolan Porterfield is a complete and evocative portrayal of the irrepressible Singing Brakeman.

Research also included the PBS American Experience documentary *The Carter Family: Will the Circle be Unbroken* and a DVD release, *Winding Stream: The Carters, The Cashes and The Course of Country Music.*

A LOOK AT: THE STEPHEN MERTZ ACTION PACK (VOLUME 1)

Three missions. Three heroes. One unforgettable collection.

Prepare for a pulse-pounding journey through history's most dangerous missions in this explosive three-book collection by acclaimed thriller writer Stephen Mertz. If you're a fan of action-packed espionage and high-stakes military drama, this is the collection you've been waiting for.

This collection includes: *Blood Red Sun, Dragon Games,* and *The Castro Directive.*

Dive into The Stephen Mertz Action Pack (Vol 1) and experience the heart-stopping thrillers that define a genre.

AVAILABLE NOW

ABOUT THE AUTHOR

Stephen Mertz was an American fiction author best known for his mainstream thrillers and novels of suspense. His work covered a wide variety of styles from paranormal dark suspense (*Night Wind* and *Devil Creek*) to historical speculative thrillers (*Blood Red Sun*) and hardboiled noir (*Fade to Tomorrow*). Mertz was also a popular lecturer on the craft of writing and appeared as a guest speaker before writer's groups and at universities.

Mertz's writing output increased dramatically when he emerged as one of the country's most in-demand writers of adventure paperback novels, averaging four books per year for ten years. His work on Don Pendleton's Mack Bolan series is regarded by fans as some of the best in that series. He also created the Mark Stone: MIA Hunter and Cody's Army series, written under the pseudonyms Jack Buchanan and Jim Case respectively.

Mertz passed away in 2024.